# "You're pre _____"

It was a questi _____
statement. Jess _____
speak, couldn't _____
her ears was too loud, and even as she
maintained her horrified silence she knew
that it pronounced the truth of what Bruno
had just said.

"Why don't you just admit it?" Bruno
raked his fingers through his hair. "You're
resigning because you're carrying my baby.
Did you have any intention of telling me?"

"Please go," Jessica begged softly.

"I'm not leaving until you tell me the truth."

"It's true. I'm pregnant...."

**She's sexy,
successful...
and
PREGNANT!**

Relax and enjoy our fabulous series about
spirited women and gorgeous men, whose
passion results in pregnancies...sometimes
unexpected! Of course, the birth of a baby is
always a joyful event, and we can guarantee that
our characters will become besotted moms and
dads—but what happened in those nine
months before?

Share the surprises, emotions, dramas and
suspense as our parents-to-be come to terms
with the prospect of bringing a new little life into
the world.... All will discover that the business of
making babies brings with it the most special
love of all....

Look out next month for:
**Having Leo's Child** (#2050)
by Emma Darcy

# CATHY WILLIAMS

## The Baby Verdict

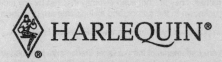

TORONTO • NEW YORK • LONDON
AMSTERDAM • PARIS • SYDNEY • HAMBURG
STOCKHOLM • ATHENS • TOKYO • MILAN • MADRID
PRAGUE • WARSAW • BUDAPEST • AUCKLAND

ISBN 0-373-12048-6

THE BABY VERDICT

First North American Publication 1999.

Look us up on-line at: http://www.romance.net

Printed In U.S.A.

# CHAPTER ONE

'THE big boss wants to see you.'

Jessica looked at the petite, blonde secretary she shared with her boss, Robert Grange, and grinned.

'Has anyone told you that you're wasted as a secretary, Millie? You have a special talent for making the most innocuous statements sound dramatic. Really, you need to be in a TV soap.' She rested her briefcase on the ground next to her and began riffling through the post, sifting out bits, leaving some for her secretary to open. 'That tax information I need still hasn't come through,' she said distractedly, ripping open an envelope and glancing through the contents. 'Why can't people get their act together? I asked for that information two days ago.'

'Jess,' her secretary said, 'you're not hearing me. You've been summoned! You need to get your skates on and not stand there flicking through the mail!'

Jessica looked up from what she was doing and frowned. 'I'm due to see Robert in fifteen minutes' time,' she said. 'What's the problem?'

'The problem is,' Millie told her in a long-suffering voice, 'you're thinking of the wrong big boss. Bruno Carr is in your office waiting for you.'

'Bruno Carr?' She glanced along the corridor. 'What does Bruno Carr want with *me?*' She had been working at BC Holdings for nine months, and during that time she had not once laid eyes on the legendary Bruno Carr. BC Holdings was just one of a multitude of companies he owned. His headquarters were in the City somewhere, and he rarely deigned to visit some of his smaller companies. Once a month, Robert would journey to the City with a case bulging with documents, proof that profits were where they should be, finances were running smoothly and employees were doing what they should be doing.

'I have no idea,' Millie said now, throwing a cursory glance at her perfectly shaped nails, today painted jade-green to match the colours of her suit, 'but he doesn't look like the kind of man who appreciates being kept waiting.'

Well, what kind of man *does* he look like? Jessica wanted to ask. She felt a thread of nervous tension snake through her body and she did a quick mental calculation of what she might possibly have done to warrant Bruno Carr descending on her.

'You should have *asked* him what he wanted,' she hissed, her brown eyes flicking between the corridor and her secretary. 'That's what secretaries are *for.*' She was very rarely thrown off balance by anything, but the sudden unexpectedness of this was enough to disconcert her.

'People don't ask Bruno Carr questions like that!' Millie exclaimed in a horrified voice. 'He comes in, says what he wants, and you just nod a lot and do it.'

'Well, he sounds a particularly pleasant kind of individual.'

A great, big, overweight, pompous man who went around stamping on the little people and issuing orders by royal decree. This was all she needed on a freezing January Monday morning.

'Where's Robert?' she asked, postponing the inevitable for as long as she could. Her lawyer's instinct told her to get as much information about what was going on as she possibly could, even if Millie was being particularly unforthcoming.

'Meeting. He was told to go ahead without you.'

'I see.'

'Guess that means that the great Bruno Carr wants to see you all on your lonesome,' she whispered confidentially. 'Sounds ominous, if you ask me.'

'I don't recall asking you,' Jessica said automatically. 'Well, I'd better go along in.' Whatever it was she had done, it had clearly been a grave crime against Bruno Carr's enterprises, for which she was to be punished by immediate dismissal. Perhaps she had inadvertently taken home one of the company's red marker pens with her, and he had somehow discovered it. From the sound of it, he was just the sort of man who would see that as reason for instant sacking. And why else would he have sought her out, making sure that he gave no warning in advance, if not to confront her with some misdemeanour?

She retrieved her briefcase from the ground and mentally braced herself for the worst.

'Could you bring us in some coffee in about ten minutes' time, Mills?' she asked, running her hands along her neatly pinned back blonde hair, just to make sure that there were no loose strands waiting to ambush her composure.

'You mean if Mr Carr allows it...'

'You're being ridiculous now.'

She pulled herself erect and headed down the corridor, pausing briefly outside her door and wondering whether she should knock or not. There was no remote reason why she should knock to enter her own office, but, then again, barging in might be another nail in her coffin.

It was frustrating. She could admit, without any false modesty, that although she had been at the company for under a year she was doing a brilliant job. She had a sharp, alert mind and a willingness to work any number of hours to get a job done. What could he possibly have found to criticise in her performance?

She found herself knocking angrily on the door, then she pushed it open and walked in.

He was sitting in *her* chair, which was turned away from the door so that only the top of his head was visible, because he was talking on *her* phone, his voice low and staccato. She stood for a few seconds, glaring at the back of the leather swivel chair, knowing how those bears had felt when Goldilocks had swanned in in their absence and usurped their property.

'Excuse me. Mr Carr?' she said, folding her arms and injecting as much crispness into her tone as was possible, just in case some of her annoyance oozed out.

He turned around very slowly and she stared at him, mouth open, as he slowly finished his telephone conversation and leant forward to replace the phone. Then he sat back, folded his arms, and looked at her without saying anything.

She had been expecting thinning grey hair. She had been expecting middle-aged spread caused by too many rich lunches and not enough exercise. She had been expecting bushy eyebrows, wobbling jowls and a tightly pursed mouth.

Why had the wretched Millicent given her no warning of what the man looked like?

True, there was arrogance stamped on those hard features, but any arrogance was well contained in a face that was the most powerfully sensual she had ever seen in her life before.

His hair was almost black, his eyes shrewd, cool, and wintry blue and the lines of his face were perfectly chiselled, yet somehow escaping from the category of routinely handsome.

Handsome, Jessica thought, was a combination of features that blended well together. Perhaps it was his expression and a certain mantle of accepted self-assurance, or maybe it was the overall impression of brains and power, but there was some intangible element to the man sitting in front of her that catapulted him into a category all of his own.

'What are you doing in my chair?' she asked stupidly, forcing down the immediate physical impact he had made on her and trying to retrieve some of her composure back from where it had been flung to the four winds.

'*Your* chair?' His voice was low, velvety and coldly ironic.

She instantly felt her hackles rise. It was easy to work out what his type was: the wealthy, clever, powerful, good-looking bachelor who assumed that the world lay somewhere in the region of his feet.

'Sorry. I meant *your* chair in my office.' She smiled sweetly and continued to look at him with a steady, unfaltering gaze.

Her momentary lapse at being confronted with such intense masculinity had now been put away in a box at the back of her mind, and her self-control was once again reasserting itself.

It never let her down. It had been her companion for such a long time, seemingly all twenty-eight years of her life, that she could avail herself of it effortlessly.

He didn't bother to answer that. Instead, he nodded briefly in the direction of the chair facing him, and told her to sit down.

'I've been waiting to see you for the past...' he flicked back the cuff of his shirt and consulted the gold watch '...twenty-five minutes. Do you normally get into work this late?'

Jessica sat down, crossed her legs and swallowed down the lump of anger in her throat.

'My hours are nine to five—' she began.

'Clock watching isn't a trait I encourage in my employees.'

'But I left work at a little after ten last night. If I got in at a little after nine, then I do apologise. I'm normally up and running here by eight-thirty in the morning.' She bared her teeth in a semblance of politeness and linked her fingers together on one knee.

'Robert sings your praises...' he looked at the piece of paper lying in front of him, which she recognised, upside down, as her CV '...Jessica. I take it, by the way, that you know who I am?'

'Bruno Carr,' she said, tempted to add *Leader of the Universe.*

'You're younger than I imagined from what Robert has told me,' he said flatly. He looked at her speculatively through narrowed eyes, as if weighing her up, and she wondered what her age had to do with the price of sliced bread. Instead, she thought, of making disparaging comments on her age, why didn't he just cut to the nub of the matter and tell her why he was here? In her office, sitting in her chair, having used her telephone.

'Would you mind very much if I had a cup of coffee? Before I launch into defending my age?' That one she couldn't resist, and he raised his eyebrows, unamused.

'Millie,' he buzzed, 'two coffees, please.' He leaned back into the chair, which dwarfed her even though she was tall, but appeared made for him. Even though he was camouflaged by his suit, she could see that he had a muscular, athletic physique and was tall. He would be, she reckoned, one of those rarities: a man she would have to look up to, even when she was in heels.

In record time there was a knock at the door and Millie fluttered in with a tray, on which were two cups, with saucers, instead of the usual mugs, a plate of biscuits and cream and sugar.

'Will there be anything else?' she asked, smiling coyly and hovering.

Oh, please, Jessica thought wryly. Was this the same delicate, porcelain girl who could make mincemeat of men? Bruno's presence had obviously reduced her to the archetypal eyelash-batting, empty-headed bimbo she most certainly was not. No wonder the man wore that aura of invincibility about him, if women dropped like ninepins every time he was around.

'For the moment.' He looked appreciatively at a blushing Millie and gave a smile of such profound sensual charm that Jessica's breath caught in her throat for the merest fleeting of seconds. Then she steadied herself and reached forward for the cup on the tray.

Yes, men like Bruno Carr were a dangerous species. The sort who should carry health warnings stamped on their foreheads so that women knew to steer clear of them.

Jessica's mouth tightened as her mind flicked through the pages of her past, like a calendar blown back by a strong wind.

She remembered her father, tall, elegant, charming, always talking to her mother's friends, making them feel special. It was only later, as she had grown up, that she had realised that his activities had extended well beyond merely talking and that his charm, never applied to his wife, had been only skin-deep.

'Now,' he said, once Millie had disappeared out of the door, 'you're doubtless wondering why I'm here.'

'It's crossed my mind.' After all, she thought acidly, it's hardly been your policy in the past to fraternise. At least not with the members of *this* particular offshoot company, however hugely profitable it was.

'Has Robert said anything to you about his health?' Bruno asked, leaning forward with his elbows on the desk.

'About his *health*?' Jessica looked at him, confused. 'No. Why? Is there something wrong?' She knew that over the past three months he had been leaving work earlier than usual, but he had told her that a man of his age needed to wind down eventually, and she had believed him.

'Have you noticed *nothing* about his hours recently?' There was cool sarcasm in his voice and she stiffened.

'He hasn't been working very much overtime...'

'And he's been delegating quite a substantial amount of his workload onto you. Am I right?'

'A bit,' she admitted, wondering why she had never questioned that.

'And yet you didn't put two and two together? Hardly a very positive trait in a lawyer. Shouldn't lawyers be adept at ferrying out information and making assumptions?'

'I apologise if I didn't see anything sinister in his behaviour,' she said with equal coldness in her voice. 'Believe it or not, cross-examining my boss wasn't part of my job specification.' She could feel her anger going up a notch and was alarmed more by the fact that he had managed to arouse such a reaction in her than by what he had said.

Outbursts of emotions were not something that she was accustomed to dealing with. From a young age, as she had stood on the sidelines and watched the antics of her father and the misery of her long-suffering mother, she had learned to control her emotions, to keep them under lock and key.

'Are you telling me that he's ill?' she asked tightly, worry in her voice.

'Stomach ulcer. He's on medication for it and has been for a while, but he's now been told that he needs to have a sabbatical. At least six months away from the stress of a work environment.'

'How dreadful. I wish he'd said something to me. I would have relieved him of far more of his workload.' She thought of her boss—tall, grey-haired, kindly, always encouraging her and never backward in his praise when she'd done a good job at something—and felt a stab of guilt.

Bruno was right. *Why* hadn't she put two and two together and worked out that he was not well?

'It's unfortunate,' Bruno said, watching her face and reading her reaction, 'but it's not terminal.'

'I'm afraid I don't know a great deal about stomach ulcers...'

'I gathered that from the expression on your face.' He raked his fingers through his hair, and she watched, half mesmerised by this simple gesture.

'I've told him,' Bruno said, 'that the sooner he leaves the better. There's no point jeopardising his health for the sake of a job. Which,' he continued slowly, 'brings me to you, and the reason I'm here.'

'Right. Of course.' She was still dazedly thinking of all the signs she had missed over the past few months.

'You're Robert's second in command. I gather that you're good at your job.'

What did he expect her to say to that? 'I do my best.'

'I've read your CV. For someone who's so young, you appear to have excelled in your previous job, and in your law exams.'

*Appear to have excelled?* What was he trying to tell her? That he doubted what was in front of him?

'Why didn't you go down the line of barrister?' he asked, not looking at her, still flicking through the sheets of paper in front of him.

'I thought about it,' Jessica said, still smarting from his

tone of voice. 'In the end, I decided that working within a company would give me more of a sense of stability and fulfilment. Of course, I still have friends in the field of criminal law and I try and go to as many court cases as I can.'

'As a hobby?' He glanced up at her, his eyes unreadable, and she wondered whether there was an element of sarcasm there.

'It's as useful a *hobby* as any I can think of,' she said a little sharply.

'Useful...if a little solitary.'

'Which is no bad thing, as far as I am concerned.'

He looked at her fully then, not saying anything for such a long time that she began to feel uncomfortable. Then he pushed himself away from the desk and stood up, his hands in his pockets, and began pacing the room, finally ending up by the window, where he remained standing, resting back against the ledge.

He was even taller than she had originally thought, and his body had a toned leanness to it that reminded her of something dangerous and unpredictable. Some kind of predatory jungle animal. Or perhaps, she thought, aware that she shouldn't stare and therefore carefully averting her eyes to a point slightly to the side of him, that was simply the overall impression he emanated.

'You'll have to cover for Robert during his absence,' he said, looking at her, his blue eyes calculating. 'Naturally, you'll be financially compensated.'

'That won't be a problem.' She could hardly carry on talking to the upper-left angle of the window, so she looked him fully in the face, and felt that disturbing awareness again.

Whatever was wrong with her? She didn't even care for the man! He was about as jovial as a barracuda. Not the sort of man she went for at all. Her boyfriends, short-lived though they tended to be, were all fashioned in the same mould: easygoing, considerate, occasionally a little dull. But men she could handle.

She had seen firsthand how debilitating it could be to live a life over which you exercised no control. She had watched her mother wither over the years as she had endured her husband's brutal infidelities, tied to the house because she had been told repeatedly that she was incapable of doing anything on her own.

Jessica had fashioned her escape from that stifling atmosphere with the precision of a military campaign. While her teenaged friends had spent their days swooning over boys and experimenting with make-up, she had buried her head in her books, working with the single-minded passion of someone who needed to furiously dig a tunnel before they could see the outside world.

She had no intention of ever handing over control of her life to someone else. She had studied hard, worked hard and every step of her career had been built on determination and lessons learnt in the past.

'I already work very closely with Robert, anyway,' she said, snapping back to the present and focusing on the man standing in front of her. 'I know most of his client base. The rest I can familiarise myself with easily enough.' A temporary promotion. She breathed a little sigh of relief. And to think that she had hovered uncertainly by that office door, convinced that she was about to be handed her walking cards.

'Will that be all?' she asked, standing up. She smiled and extended her hand.

'No.'

'I beg your pardon?'

'No, that will not be all, so you might as well sit back down.'

A man accustomed to giving orders. A man who by-passed the polite preliminaries of conversation that most people took for granted.

She withdrew her hand, feeling a bit idiotic, and sat back down.

'You don't think that I travelled out here merely to inform you that you've got a promotion, do you?' His voice was cool and amused, and it was an effort for her to continue looking at him without dislike.

'I know,' she said, 'that was silly of me, wasn't it?'

He frowned, and she struggled to contain a sudden urge to grin.

'Do I hear a little edge of sarcasm there?' he asked mildly.

'Of course not!' Her brown eyes were innocently shocked at such a suggestion. 'I wouldn't dare!'

'You haven't asked when Robert is due to leave.' He returned to the chair behind the desk, sat back down and then pushed it away so that he could cross his legs, ankle on knee.

'I assumed...' What had she assumed? 'I guessed that it would be in a couple of months' time...?'

'At the end of the week.'

'The end of the week!' Jessica looked at him, startled. 'The end of *this* week? But how? Why hasn't he said anything to me? Surely he'll need longer than four days to tie up loose ends...'

'Are you beginning to regret your optimism in filling in for him?'

'I'm just expressing surprise at the suddenness of it all,' she told him coldly. 'I'm also a little bit taken aback that he didn't see fit to inform me before this.'

'You have me to thank for that,' he said bluntly. 'This development happened overnight, literally, and I told him that it would be better for me to talk to you. In fact, it was essential that I did.' He paused, as though contemplating what to say next. 'His mother lives in America and two days ago she suffered a stroke. I told him that it made sense for him to combine his leave with a visit out there to see her. He'll speak to you about this when he gets in this afternoon, then he'll call a staff meeting some time tomorrow.'

'I see.'

'The reason I made a point of coming out here to tell you all this yourself—'

'When you almost certainly would have had better things to do,' Jessica muttered to herself.

'Sorry? I missed that.' He leaned forward slightly, and she flashed him a brilliant smile.

'Nothing important. Just thinking aloud.'

'This sudden development comes at a rather inconvenient time.'

'Inconvenient for whom?' she asked.

'I'll ignore that question,' Bruno told her, narrowing his eyes. 'It borders on impertinence.'

Which it did. She felt colour steal into her cheeks. Had she forgotten that this man was her boss? Had she forgotten that she should toe the line and not risk her career for the sake of emotion?

'I'm sorry,' she said honestly. 'I suppose I'm just shocked and worried about Robert. It's been sprung on me out of the blue.'

What a limp lettuce of an excuse, she thought. She could feel his shrewd eyes on her, assessing, and she waited for him to inform her that sarcasm was not something he would tolerate. Sarcasm, she suspected, was not something he had probably ever had to deal with.

He chose to disregard what she had said, though.

'Two days ago,' he said instead, 'I received this.' He withdrew a letter from his jacket pocket and shoved it across the desk to her, then he sat back and watched while she opened it and read the contents several times over.

Bruno Carr was being sued. Personally. A component for a car, manufactured by one of his plants, had resulted in a near-fatal car crash.

'This,' he explained softly, 'is why I thought it important to come and see you myself.'

Jessica looked up briefly before re-reading the official letter. 'To see if you considered me capable of dealing with this...'

'That's right. And you're not what I expected.'

'Is that why you expressed concern about my age, Mr Carr?' She carefully placed the sheet of paper on the desk in front of her and sat back, with her fingers linked on her lap.

A legal issue was something she could deal with. The personal confrontation with Bruno Carr had brought out feelings in her she hadn't even known existed, at least not for a very long time. But this. She took her time considering him.

'You think that because I'm relatively young I'm incapable of doing a good job.'

'You lack experience,' he said flatly. 'You are also a woman.'

'Perhaps I could address those concerns of yours one at a time?' When she smiled, her jaw ached because of the effort, and her fingers werc itching to hurl something very heavy at him. Precisely what century was this man living in?

'Firstly, age has nothing to do with competence. I can't deny that I haven't got three decades' worth of experience behind me, but then I can assure you that I am more than capable of dealing with this lawsuit.' The only way to deal with Bruno Carr, she decided, was not to be cowed by him. He would smell out any hint of uncertainty from her with the unerring precision of a shark smelling blood, and he would promptly take his lawsuit somewhere else. Careerwise, it would be death for her.

'Of course, I shall need immediate and unrestricted access to any information, technical or otherwise, that I consider necessary...'

He nodded fractionally, and continued to look at her, waiting for her to say her piece, upon which he would deliver his verdict.

'Fine. Now, secondly, yes, I am a woman.' Camouflaged as it was by her genderless working garb. In a man's world, frilly dresses were off limits—not that she had ever been one for frilly dresses anyway. A suit told the world precisely what she wanted it to know, which was that she was to be taken seriously. Even outside the working environment, she steered clear of frocks and short skirts, preferring jeans and clothes that were tailored and smart rather than provocative. It was only when she stripped at night that she saw the reflection of her own body in the mirror—tall, slender, but with full breasts and long legs. A good figure, she knew. It was as well to conceal it.

'However,' she continued, 'women comprise a high percentage of the working arena these days, in case you hadn't noticed. I'm sure if you cast your eyes around you'll discover that there are quite a few spread throughout your various companies.'

'Ah, but none of them is poised to defend my name in a lawsuit, are they?' he pointed out smoothly.

'And why do you think that a man might be more competent at the job than a woman?' she asked, changing tactic. She fixed him a cool, implacable stare, one of her specialities when it came to withering any member of the opposite sex who might be overstepping her boundaries. He stared back at her, unperturbed.

'Because women are prone to outbursts of hysteria when the going gets too tough, and I, frankly, don't think that that will do at all in this instance.'

Oh, good grief, Jessica thought to herself. *Was she really hearing this?*

'Outbursts of hysteria?' she asked politely, with her head tilted to one side. 'When the going gets tough?' She laughed dryly. 'Possibly with the women you tend to associate with, but I can assure you that there's a whole army of them out there who don't react in any such way when faced with a challenge.' She paused, and added for good measure, 'And by challenge I don't mean colour co-ordinating our clothes or debating what shade of nail polish we should wear on our next date.'

He looked away and she caught something that looked remarkably like a stifled smile, although she couldn't be sure, because when he once again looked at her his face was serious.

'Robert has every confidence in your ability,' he told her. 'And that's counted heavily in your favour. If it were up to me, I would say that a young, inexperienced woman would not come high on the list of people I would choose to handle this.'

I'm going to have to work fairly closely with this man if I get this job, Jessica thought grimly. I'm going to have to quell the urge to strangle him.

'Well,' she informed him with a cool little smile and a slight shrug, 'there's nothing more I can say to convince you that I'd do a good job. If you don't feel one hundred per cent confident of my abilities, then, of course, you must look elsewhere.'

The interview, as far as she was concerned, was finished, but she was deeply reluctant to stand up, just in case he ordered her to sit back down again.

He saved her the decision by standing up himself and moving around the desk towards her.

For a second she felt a recurrence of that vague, unspecified alarm that had wrong-footed her previously, then it subsided and she rose to her feet. In her heels, she reached just to the level of his mouth, and she averted her eyes hurriedly because, almost unconsciously, her mind registered that it was a disconcertingly sensual mouth.

'I'm prepared to give you the benefit of the doubt, Miss Stearn,' he said, reaching out to shake her hand.

'And I'm flattered,' she replied, withdrawing her hand almost immediately, 'especially since I realise that it goes against your better judgement. I'll do a good job.'

'Oh, I hope so,' he drawled, looking down at her, 'for both our sakes.'

'Quite.' She abandoned all attempts at smiling. Why bother? If he could be brutally frank with her, then she would be as brutally frank back, within reasonable limits.

'And I feel I should warn you that I'm intolerant of incompetence, especially when my reputation is at stake.'

'Thanks for the warning. I'll bear it in mind.'

She watched as he walked towards the door, then as he was about to open it he turned and looked at her over his shoulder.

'You're quite the hard nut, aren't you?' he said in a speculative voice.

Was he surprised? She supposed so. Quite unexpectedly, she had a vision of the sort of women he appreciated, and she could guarantee that not a single hard nut would be among them.

'I'm not about to agree or disagree with that, Mr Carr. You're entitled to your own opinion.'

He nodded, half smiled, and then closed the door behind him, and it was only then, as her body sagged, that she realised quite how much strain she had been under.

The news about Robert had come as a shock. He had seemed fit enough. Hadn't he? She frowned and tried to remember whether there had been any give-away signs of ill health. Then, uneasily, it crossed her mind that perhaps there had been and she had just failed to recognise them because she'd been so wrapped up in her work. Her concentration on her job was single-minded and complete, which, she acknowledged, was great when it came to climbing ladders and winning promotions, but there was a great big world out there and...was it passing her by?

No. Surely not. She had a successful, rewarding career. How could anything be passing her by? Every goal she had striven for had been achieved. She should feel nothing but satisfaction.

Of course, her love life was not exactly thrilling. In fact, it was positively non-existent at the moment. Her relationship with Greg had ended six months ago, which had been roughly its duration. She uncomfortably remembered his criticism of her—that she had been obsessed with her career.

*You're quite the hard nut, aren't you?*

There's nothing wrong with wanting to be independent, she told herself fiercely. If her mother had been financially independent, she would have had the courage to leave the man who had made her life hell.

There's nothing wrong with me, she thought, and, if it's the last thing I do, I'll prove that I can take this case and win it.

# CHAPTER TWO

JESSICA looked at her watch, stretched, and debated whether she should telephone Bruno Carr or not. It was eight o'clock, she was still at work, and she needed information. If she was to win this case, she thought with a sense of self-righteous indignation, then he would have to be more available to answer questions. For the past week he had been abroad on business, and, however much information she could gather from various members of various departments, sooner or later he would have to avail himself.

She eyed the phone warily, as though fearing that it might metamorphose into something unpleasant at any moment, then, making her mind up, she dialled his direct work extension and was on the verge of hanging up when she heard his voice down the other end.

Irrationally, she felt a flutter of nerves.

'Mr Carr? This is Jessica Stearn here. I've been trying to reach you for the past week, but I gather you've been away on business.'

'New York.'

'Well, I'm glad you're back because there are one or two questions I need to ask you.' She shuffled some bits of paper in front of her, then began to doodle on her notepad.

'Fire away.'

'I think it might be better if this is done face to face. It's important that you familiarise yourself with every aspect of the case so that every question that's thrown at you on the stand can be dealt with.'

'It wasn't my intention to go into the witness box unprepared,' he said dryly.

'Perhaps we could meet some time tomorrow?' she asked, glancing at her diary.

'Why not now?'

'Now?'

'I take it you're still at work.'

'Yes, I am, but—'

'No time like the present. Now, do you know the address of my office here?' He rattled it off, and she hurriedly scribbled it alongside her complicated doodle. 'Get a cab. You'll get here quicker.'

'Yes, but—'

She heard the flat hum of the dialling tone and stared at the receiver in her hand with an expression of stunned amazement. He'd hung up on her! He'd decided that now was as good a time to answer questions as any, and hadn't even had the common politeness to ask her what her plans for the evening might be!

Was he so used to getting his own way that he simply took it for granted that the rest of the human race would fall in with whatever he wanted?

She stood up, slipped on her jacket and coat, grabbed her handbag from the low, square table in the corner of her office and hurried out of the building.

The more she thought about his attitude, the more exasperated she became. She could very nearly convince herself that she had really had exciting plans for the evening, when in fact her plans had included no more than a quick, pre-prepared meal in front of the television, a few law articles she wanted to have a look at, and then bed.

Hardly heady stuff, she knew, but she had been working since eight-thirty in the morning, and a low-key evening was just what she felt she needed.

It didn't help that she had to trudge two blocks and wait
fifteen minutes before she managed to hail a taxi. Thursday
nights were always busy. Late-night shopping and the remnants of the January sales were enough to encourage even
the laziest into the streets. She watched as taxi after taxi
trundled past and was in a thoroughly foul temper by the
time a vacant one pulled over to the side for her.

I need a long soak in a bath, she fumed silently to herself,
staring out of the window at the bright lights and the people, hurrying along to minimise the length of time they
spent in the cold. Her suit felt starched and uncomfortable,
her make-up had almost vanished completely and she
wanted to kick off her shoes and let her feet breathe.

His office block in the City was quite different from
where she worked. Large, with a lot of opaque glass everywhere, and, when she entered, a profusion of plants
strewn around an enormous reception area, in the centre of
which the large, circular desk, manned by an elderly man
in uniform, was a bit like an island adrift in the middle of
an ocean.

A group of three men in suits was standing to one side,
talking in low voices, and they glanced around automatically as she entered the building, but aside from them it
was empty.

Because, she thought, everyone else has left to go home
and relax, or else get dressed before stepping out to paint
the town red.

Jessica couldn't remember the last time she had painted
the town red. She had a sneaking suspicion that she had
never painted it red—or any other colour, come to think of
it.

During her more active moments, when she'd been involved with a man, few and far between though they had
been, she had gone to the theatre or had meals out.

Somehow, she didn't think that that fell into the 'Red Paint' category.

'Mr Carr, please,' she said to the man behind the desk, now feeling gloomy in addition to exasperated and inconvenienced.

He lifted the receiver, spoke for a few seconds, and then nodded at her.

'Mr Carr's expecting you,' he said, and she resisted the impulse to tell him that she knew that already, considering she had been summoned half an hour ago. 'Fourth floor, last office on the right. He said it'll be fine for you to make your own way up.'

'Oh, grand!' Jessica said with a large, beaming smile. 'That must mean that he trusts me not to nick anything *en route*.'

She was standing outside his office door at a little after eight-thirty, quietly determined that she would stay no longer than half an hour. Long enough to brief him on the details of the case, find out his thoughts firsthand, and then anything more detailed could be arranged via their secretaries.

That way, she would be back at her apartment in North London by ten at the latest, just in time to catch the news, microwave a meal and read for half an hour. Any law books would have to wait for another day.

The thick, mahogany door was slightly ajar, so she knocked and pushed it open without waiting for a reply. The room, obviously his secretary's, was empty. Jessica glanced around it, unconsciously noting that it was larger than most of the top directors' offices she had been into in her lifetime, if a little lacking in character. A comfortable, functional room that spoke of high-octane efficiency and an ability to get on with the job without distraction.

She strode purposefully towards a further interconnecting

door, knocked and, without thinking, pushed it open. He had been expecting her, hadn't he?

Obviously not, because he was not alone, and his companion was not a fellow senior worker who might have popped in for a five-minute chat. Not unless his fellow senior workers resembled Barbie dolls.

'I—I'm sorry,' Jessica stammered, embarrassed, 'I had no idea that I was interrupting...'

'Come in.'

Bruno looked not in the least disconcerted by her abrupt arrival. His female companion, however, clearly didn't welcome the intrusion. She turned from where she was half sitting on his desk and looked at Jessica with no attempt to disguise her annoyance.

'You could have knocked,' was her opening line. Her voice, high and girlish, matched the rest of her. She was the perfect male fantasy package. Jessica acknowledged that without a trace of envy. Petite, curvy, with full breasts bursting out of a tight-fitting, long-sleeved top, a skirt that was short enough to leave little to the imagination, and high shoes, which had been discarded. The blonde hair hung in curls past her shoulders and her face was angelic, even if the expression on it wasn't.

'I didn't expect...' Jessica began, not quite knowing where to go from there.

'You never said that your so-called meeting was with a woman!' the girl accused Bruno, pouting.

'I think it's time you left, Rachel,' he said, patting her arm to encourage her off the desk.

'But we need to talk! You promised!' She wriggled unhappily off the desk and stepped into her shoes. Her face was a mixture of frustration and pleading.

'Perhaps you could come over to my place when you're

finished here.' She turned to Jessica. 'You won't be long,
will you?'

'No, I don't plan—'

'Close the door behind you after you leave, Rachel,'
Bruno interrupted, swerving back behind the desk and tapping into his computer.

Oh, charming, Jessica thought. Was this how he treated
all his women? She edged into the room, uncomfortably
watching as the dismissed blonde stormed out of the office,
slamming the door behind her, then she sat down facing
him and placed a sheaf of papers on the desk between them.

'I won't keep you,' she said icily. 'I had rather planned
one or two things this evening...'

'Oh, really? What?' He looked up from the computer
with a mildly curious expression.

This was not what she had expected. Fool that she was,
she had anticipated some sort of apology, if only for the
sake of politeness.

TV, a microwave dinner and an early night did not seem
the appropriate admission. However, she could not bring
herself to tell an outright lie. Instead, she said, 'I need to
consult a couple of references in some law books at
home...'

'Another fascinating hobby of yours, is it?' The blue
eyes glinted with sardonic humour. 'I shudder to think what
your dull moments are comprised of.'

Oh, what a keen sense of humour, she thought acidly,
excuse me if I don't fall off my chair laughing.

How could she have forgotten quite how irritating the
man was?

'I've read every detail of the case that's being put forward,' she said, ignoring his remark completely and tapping
the sheaf of papers on the desk. 'And I've highlighted the
areas we particularly need to concentrate on.'

He obligingly picked up the lot, scanned through them, replaced them on the desk and asked her if she had eaten.

'I beg your pardon?'

'Have you eaten? Had dinner? Consumed food within the last three hours?'

'I know what you mean,' Jessica snapped, 'I just have no idea why you're asking.'

'It's late. I think we might just as well go out for a quick bite. We can go through all this tomorrow when we're feeling more alert.'

'You're kidding, aren't you?' But he didn't seem to be. She watched, bewildered, as he strolled across to the two-seater sofa by the bookshelf, picked up his jacket and slung it on, followed by a camel-coloured trenchcoat.

'There's a good Italian just around the corner. I can always get a table there.' He stopped to look at her. 'Coming?'

'This is ridiculous,' Jessica spluttered, getting to her feet and feeling utterly manipulated as she shoved all the paperwork back into her briefcase. 'With all due respect, this has been a pointless exercise for me.'

'Oh, I don't know,' he mused, eyebrows raised, 'a meal out is surely more fun than looking up a few legal references...'

'I would say that depends entirely on the company involved,' she muttered stiffly.

'If it's any consolation, we'll talk business for the duration of the meal. How about that?' His phoney, soothing tone of voice got on her nerves even more, and she took a few deep breaths and controlled her temper.

'I'm not dressed for a meal out,' she pointed out, because a wayward thought had suddenly crossed her mind: she didn't want to be alone with Bruno Carr unless there was the reassuring presence of files, desks and computers around.

'Oh, I don't know.' He gave her a leisurely look. 'I'm sure Gino has witnessed the sight of a working woman in a suit before. This *is* the twentieth century, after all, as you were so adamant about pointing out the last time we met.'

He opened the door, stood aside, and she brushed past him with a lofty expression. Diplomacy is the better part of valour, she told herself on the way down in the lift. She was doing this because he was her boss and refusing point-blank was hardly a tactful manoeuvre. If any other man had treated her with such high-handed arrogance, she would have dismissed him on the spot.

That was a comforting thought.

They walked quickly and in silence to the restaurant. In this part of London, there were fewer people about. There were no trendy boutiques to attract the shoppers and not enough fashionable clubs to entice the young and the beautiful.

It was also too cold for dawdling. Within ten minutes they were at the restaurant, which was surprisingly full with an after-work crowd, but the proprietor immediately recognised Bruno and showed them to a table in the furthest corner of the place.

It occurred to Jessica that his girlfriend, or lover, or whoever the small, well-endowed blonde was, would not be impressed to find that his important business meeting had translated itself into a meal at the local Italian.

A suspicious thought began playing at the back of her mind, but she lost it as they were handed menus and the dishes of the day were explained with elaborate, Mediterranean flamboyance.

She had meals out with girlfriends on a fairly regular basis, but it had been a while since she had had a meal out with a man, and against all better judgement she found herself sneaking glances at Bruno as he contemplated the menu in front of him and ordered a bottle of white wine.

It was a unique experience to walk into a room and know that female heads were surreptitiously turning in their direction as they watched and assessed from under lowered lashes. She did not have the immediately captivating face of someone who aroused curious second looks. She was not unattractive, but she knew, deep down, that the few attractions she did possess were played down. Her mind and intelligence were what she wanted on display, rather than her physical attributes. It felt peculiar to be speculated upon by perfect strangers, even if it was simply because she was in the company of Bruno Carr.

He looked up suddenly from the menu and she dropped her eyes, ruffled to think that he might have caught her stare and followed the train of her thoughts from it.

'So,' he said lazily, 'shall we launch immediately into a work-related discussion or would you like to have a glass of wine first?'

Why did she get the impression that, although he recognised her intelligence, he was secretly laughing at her?

'I do have it in me to converse about things other than work,' she told him coldly, unsettled by his attitude. She felt as though he was toying with her, in much the same way that a cat toyed with a mouse. 'I just thought that that was my reason for flying over to see you at this time of the night.'

He ignored that part of her little speech. 'Other things than work...well, I guess that means...play?' He had ordered a bottle of white wine, and he looked at her as he tasted a thumbful, nodded, and then waited while two glasses were poured. 'So, aside from law books and court cases, what other forms of play do you indulge in?'

He tilted his head slightly to one side, sipped his wine and contemplated her with a gravity which she knew was fake. He was highly amused by her and she found it exasperating.

'I'm sure you know,' she informed him calmly, taking a mouthful of wine and savouring the taste on her tongue, 'considering you had my CV in front of you in my office and it was all listed there. But, in case you forgot, I enjoy going to the theatre, reading and foreign travel. What about you?' She looked at him without blinking and decided that two could play that game. 'Oops, sorry. I saw firsthand in your office what sort of play you enjoy indulging in.'

*Had she said that?*

*Had she gone completely mad?*

He grinned at her wickedly. 'I do enjoy going to the theatre, reading, and foreign travel as well. But I'll admit there are other, more absorbing types of play I prefer.'

'Right.' She could feel colour stealing into her cheeks, and she hurriedly drank some more wine. 'Now, shall we discuss this case? At least go over a few things? I'm sure you have a hectic schedule tomorrow and the less—'

'Dear me. Surely you can do better than that.' He shot her a surprised look. 'Just when I thought that we were going to have a little chat about these…things other than work you enjoy talking about.'

'Okay. Then let's talk about why you ordered me over to see you only to drag me out here the minute I step foot through the door.'

'Drag you out here? You have a way with words, don't you?'

'I'm sorry,' Jessica said stiffly, 'I didn't mean to appear rude.'

'Oh, feel free to speak your mind. I appreciate honesty in a person.'

'In that case, I might as well tell you that I'm a great believer in discussion. I don't like being commanded to do things. I realise that you're my boss...'

'And have the authority to tell you precisely what I want you to do...?' His voice was soft and when he drank his wine he continued to look at her over the rim of his glass.

'Theoretically.' The conversation seemed to be getting out of hand and she wondered when they had veered away from the conventional boss-employee line of chit-chat. 'You did say that you wanted me to be honest,' she said a little defensively, in anticipation of criticism.

'Oh, I know. And there's no need to look so alarmed. I'm not about to invoke the wrath of Khan on you for your temerity. After all, we *will* be working together to some extent. We might as well make sure that we can co-operate. I'm a great believer in the open forum.'

'Except for tonight.'

'Except for tonight,' he agreed, half smiling.

'Because...?' She looked at him, and tried to let that suggestion of great charm wash over her. 'Because...' Bruno Carr did things for a reason. 'You wanted me at your office...at that precise moment...because...' It suddenly clicked. 'Because you wanted to get rid of your girlfriend and my appearance was the most convenient way of doing that...am I right?'

'You have a suspicious mind,' he answered, leaning back slightly as plates of food were put in front of them, and vegetables were distributed with flourish. 'It must be the lawyer in you.'

'I don't like being used, Mr Carr.'

'Why don't you call me Bruno? I encourage first names among my employees. Good for company morale. Makes people feel more comfortable.'

'But that's an illusion, isn't it?' Jessica said in a steely voice. 'As tonight proved. You wanted me over because it was an expedient way of getting your girlfriend to leave.'

She could see that he was getting uncomfortable with her persistence but the thought of such blatant manipulation of her stuck in her throat.

'Oh, for God's sake, you're like a dog with a bone. If it makes you feel any better to hear me admit it, then, yes, you're right. You telephoned, and the idea occurred to me that an unavoidable business meeting was just what I needed.'

Jessica finished her glass of wine and it was immediately refilled.

'That's despicable.' She thought it, yes, but she was still amazed when it popped out of her mouth, almost as though any connection between thought and action had been severed. She knew that she ought to apologise. Whatever he said about first names and appreciating honesty and trying to make his employees feel comfortable, he still owned the company she worked for.

But she found it difficult not to voice her objections. She had spent too many years witnessing the price of her mother's silence.

'Why didn't you just tell the poor woman that you were tired of her?'

*'The poor woman?'* All trace of charm had disappeared from his face and he glowered at her. 'You have no idea what you're talking about when you refer to Rachel as *the poor woman*, and I have no idea why I'm bothering to elaborate on any of this with you.'

'Guilt?' she suggested. 'Guilt that I saw through your little manoeuvre? A basic sense of decency in realising that I need some kind of explanation? Even if I *am* only an employee? I wouldn't suggest this normally, but you did say that you enjoyed the open forum.'

He shook his head and raked his fingers through his hair, then he shot her a frustrated, perplexed look from under his lashes. 'So, I gather, do you,' he commented, eyebrows raised, and she smiled serenely at him.

'I'm not in the habit of being quite so outspoken—'

'Not in the habit! God, I should think you send men running in the opposite direction as fast as their legs can take them the minute you confront them with your brand of open forum chit-chat!'

Jessica went bright red and stabbed a few of the vegetables on her plate with misdirected aggression.

'This is ridiculous,' she muttered, eating a mouthful of food that now tasted like sawdust. 'All of this is beside the point. Whatever your reasons for getting me to your office, and whether I approve of them or not, the point of my being here is in my briefcase on the ground.'

'Oh, no, you don't,' he told her darkly. 'You generated this topic of conversation, and we'll finish it.'

'Like you said, you don't owe me an explanation...'

'But we'll be working together and I don't intend to spend my time being treated like some kind of inhuman monster.'

'Does it matter, just so long as we get the job done?'

'Yes, I rather think it does.'

Jessica didn't say anything. She concentrated on her food and waited for him to speak.

'And would you like to know why? Because I wouldn't want you to think that I spend my time chasing women. We'll be working together, and I can't have you feeling threatened, now, can I?' Which, she thought, neatly put her in her place.

'I feel so much better for that. Thank you for setting my anxious mind at rest.'

'Where do you get it from?'

'Get what from?'

'That special talent you have for biting sarcasm? I can't see Robert dealing all that well with that viperlike tongue of yours.'

'Robert,' Jessica informed him stoutly, 'is a sweetie.' And I'm not normally prone to biting sarcasm, she thought to herself, but then again the rest of the human race don't provoke me quite like you do.

'Oh, good grief.' He closed his knife and fork and signalled for another bottle of wine.

Had they consumed one already? She had barely noticed what she had been drinking, and, looking down, she realised that she had done justice to her plate of food, also without noticing.

'And just to clear the air,' he informed her, 'I don't walk around treating women like second-rate citizens.'

'I'm sure you don't.'

'That's right, so you can wipe that supercilious expression off your face.'

'Look, there's really no need...'

'Rachel, just for the record, started off as a bit of fun, but I discovered that she wasn't as content as I thought just to have a good time. Pretty soon, she...she...'

'Wanted more?' Jessica said helpfully.

'Oh, you're aware of the phenomenon, are you?'

'Not personally.'

'Well...' he shrugged and adopted a hangdog expression '...what can a man do?'

The blue eyes scoured her face with boyish bewilderment.

'Oh, please!' Jessica told him awkwardly, recognising that this was the essence of true charm. Bruno Carr, arrogant and self-confident that he was, would never veer into the arena of cruelty, because he genuinely liked women.

His natural instincts were to persuade, even when seduction played no part in a hidden agenda. The ability to flirt was as inherent with him as the ability to breathe. He did it without thinking, which was why he was so adept at it.

'Women.' He raised both shoulders expressively. 'Sometimes I don't think I understand them at all.'

'Really. Now I wonder why I find that so hard to believe.'

'Rachel started talking about the importance of families, of having children, the benefits of settling down.'

'Poor, misguided girl,' Jessica said without a trace of sympathy in her voice for him. 'And what a dreadful predicament for you, I'm sure. One minute, you have a willing, vivacious partner, the next minute she's gazing into jeweller shops and dropping hints about permanence.'

'I'm not the marrying sort,' he said. 'Some men are and some men aren't.'

'You mean it's all in the genes?'

'Whereas all women are. Eventually.'

'Ah. I see.' She nodded slowly. In a strange, masochistic way, and even though she still resented his high-handed behaviour and was appalled by his train of thought, she found that she was enjoying this conversation. She must be mad.

'I mean,' he said, 'you come across as being the archetypal career woman, but, if you were to be brutally honest with yourself, wouldn't you agree that when you see the odd pram being pushed you get a certain pang?'

'What kind of pang?'

'A pang of longing. Something to do with a biological clock, I gather.' He poured another glass of wine for them both.

'Well, not that I've ever recognised, but I suppose if your theory's true then I must subconsciously have that pang lurking in there somewhere.' How come the conversation was suddenly featuring her in the starring role? Her mind was feeling a little unreliable from the wine.

'And you don't?'

Jessica shook her head and frowned. 'I thought we were talking about you,' she said, thinking furiously.

'We were, but then somehow we've ended up talking about you. I think it's important to have some insight into the people who work with me.'

'You mean you enjoy prying into their lives?'

He grinned, and then laughed, and she gave him a wry smile in return.

This was beginning to feel just a little too dangerous for her liking, although she had no idea why. They were simply, at least for the moment, getting along. She got along with lots of people. Most of the human race, in fact. So why did *this* make her feel uneasy? When he raised the bottle to her glass, she shook her head and covered it with the palm of her hand.

'I've drunk enough already,' she told him honestly. 'Any more and I'll be fit for nothing in the morning. I don't have much of a head for alcohol.'

'Lack of practice?'

'Something like that.'

'You mean you don't spend the occasional night seeing the dawn rise with a glass of champagne in your hand?'

'Not routinely, no,' she said. Her hand slipped from round the rim of the glass to the stem, and she curled her fingers lightly around it, not meeting his eye.

Did *he* do that sort of thing on a regular basis? The blonde bombshell looked like the sort of woman who appreciated overblown gestures along those lines, and presumably she was merely an indication of the type of female he went out with.

'Actually,' she said, looking at him, 'I thought people only did that sort of thing in third-rate movies.'

His mouth twitched, but at least he didn't burst into laughter. She had a sneaking suspicion that if he had her remark would somehow have backfired in her face, making her appear dull and unadventurous.

'I take it you don't approve...?'

'Does it matter what I think or not? Oh, I forgot, you like to have insight into your employees. Well, as a matter of fact, I neither approve nor disapprove. I just think that it's not my style.'

'And what *is* your style?'

His voice was a low murmur and his eyes on her were suddenly intense. She felt her skin break out in a faint film of perspiration. It was the wine, of course. Between them, they had managed to drink the better part of two bottles, and that simply was not something she was accustomed to doing. One glass, yes. But virtually a bottle? She was surprised that all she saw on his face was a look of curious interest. She should rightfully be seeing three faces, all blurry, and all with different expressions.

'Work!' she told him, plucking the word from out of the blue.

'Work,' he repeated obligingly. 'I take it that my limited time on getting insight has been exhausted?'

Jessica looked at her watch and realised that they had been at the restaurant far longer than she had imagined.

'I must be getting back!' she exclaimed.

'Before the carriage turns into a pumpkin?' he asked with dry amusement.

'I don't have a carriage,' she answered, choosing to ignore any possible innuendo. 'In fact, I shall have to take a taxi back to my place. I only hope I can find one.'

'Why don't you walk back with me to the office, and I can give you a lift home?'

'That won't be necessary.' A lift home? She thought not. Whether it was the drink or not, the night seemed to have taken her onto unfamiliar ground. She had no desire to prolong the experience. Unfamiliar ground was territory she felt should be better left unexplored. She had never been able to control her background. She had watched in helpless silence as her parents had waged their unremitting cold war and as soon as she had been able to she had left, first to university, then to London. She had learned to exercise control over her life and that had always suited her.

Bruno Carr, however, was not a man who slotted easily into any sort of category she could handle.

As she reached for her briefcase and her bag she realised that the conversation between them had had all the elements of a free fall. How had that happened?

She could feel his eyes on her, and she refused to look at him, at least until she had managed to get some of her thoughts in order.

'It'll be a damned sight more convenient if I give you a lift home,' he said.

'No, thank you. Honestly.' Why was she in such a panic at the suggestion? It made sense. 'Perhaps I ought to telephone for a taxi.' She looked around her, searching for inspiration.

'Come on,' he said, signing his credit-card slip, tearing off his copy, and then standing up. 'Before you collapse in distress at the thought of getting into a car with me.'

She heard the amusement in his voice with a sinking heart. What must he think of her? Another hysterical woman, overreacting at something utterly insignificant. Hardly professional behaviour, was it?

She took a few deep breaths to steady herself.

'I must appear quite ridiculous,' she said in a calmer voice, rooting around for something sensible to say, 'but I had no idea that the evening would be this late, and...' Inspiration! 'I completely forgot that my mum was supposed to call tonight...'

'Ah. Important call, was it?'

'My sister-in-law was due to have her baby today...' Or around now, anyway. 'Mum lives in Australia with my brother and his wife,' she explained. True enough. Three weeks after her father had died, her mum, faced with sudden freedom, had taken flight to the most distant shores possible and was having a wonderful time out there. 'She'll be terribly disappointed that I wasn't at home. Anyway, the sooner I get back the better, so if you don't mind I'll just jump in a taxi and tell him to go as quickly as he can...' She knew that she was beginning to ramble, so she stopped talking and smiled brightly at him. What a pathetic excuse.

'Of course. At times like these, every second counts.' He ushered her out of the restaurant, and as luck would have it hailed a cab within seconds.

'There now,' he said, opening the door for her and peering in as she settled in the back. 'Feel better?'

She felt a complete fool, but she smiled and nodded and tried to inject an expression of relief on her face.

'Tomorrow,' he told her. 'My office. Eight-thirty.' He stood back slightly with his hand on the door. 'Make sure you bring your brain with you. You've got important work ahead of you. Can't have your head addled with thoughts of babies.' With which he slammed the door behind him, and Jessica ground her teeth together in sheer frustration and watched as he strode off along the pavement in the direction of his building.

# CHAPTER THREE

'I SHALL have to look at a drawing of the part in question. Is there any chance at all that it could have been made slightly askew? Grooves in the wrong place? Too many grooves? Too few? Anything at all that might have caused that car to malfunction?'

'Don't be ridiculous.'

Jessica sighed and looked across the table to where Bruno was sitting, his chair pushed back, his legs loosely crossed, with a stack of papers on his lap.

The boardroom was enormous, but he had insisted from the start that it was the only place that could guarantee his uninterrupted time. She still felt dwarfed by its vastness, however, and their voices had that hollow quality peculiar to when people spoke in cavernous surroundings.

'You'll be asked that in the witness box,' she said calmly, 'and I don't think that the answer you just gave me is going to do.' They had been working closely together for three weeks and this was not the first time that she had had to remind him that his answers would have to be laboriously intricate, leaving nothing to the imagination. He had a tendency to bypass all those tedious details, which he assumed everyone should know without having to be told.

'Why not?'

Jessica sighed again, this time a little louder. It was late, her eyes were stinging and she was in no mood to launch into a debate on the whys and wherefores of what could and couldn't be said on the stand. He tapped his fountain pen idly on the stack of papers and continued to look at her through narrowed eyes.

She was certain that he knew precisely how to make her feel uncomfortable. He knew that she was fine just so long as they stuck to their brief, but an errant gesture or a look that hovered just a fraction too long was enough to make her feel hot and bothered. She never showed it, but he could sense her change in mood and was not averse to preying on it for a bit of fun.

'You're being difficult,' she said at last. 'It's late. Perhaps we should wrap it up for the day.' She stood up and he followed her with his eyes, leaning back and clasping his hands together at the back of his head.

She had thought, initially, that she would become immune to his overwhelming personality and those dark, striking good looks, but she hadn't. In the middle of a question, or as he swivelled to one side when he spoke on the telephone, or even at the end of a long day, when he stretched so that his taut, muscular body flexed beneath the well-tailored suit, she could feel her eyes travel the length of his body, she could feel her mouth become suddenly dry.

Now, she dealt with her own treacherous and aggravating response to him by doing her utmost to avoid eye contact.

'*Being difficult?* Explain what you mean by *being difficult.*'

Jessica didn't answer. She walked across the room, removed her jacket and coat from the hanger and then walked back to her pile of papers. Without looking at him, she began sifting through them, pausing to read snatches of reports, then she stuffed the lot into her briefcase and snapped it shut.

'I'm tired too,' she said, meeting his stare reluctantly. 'It's been a long week.'

'You're right,' he surprised her by saying. 'Friday is the

worst day to work late. Don't you agree?' He had slung
his jacket over the back of the leather chair, and he stuck
it on, tugging his tie off and shoving it into his pocket.
Then he undid the top button of his shirt.

Jessica followed all of this with a mortifying sense of
compulsion, then she blinked and dragged her eyes away.

The end of the case couldn't come a day too soon as far
as she was concerned. Working alongside Bruno Carr was
stretching her nerves to breaking-point, and she couldn't
quite work out why.

'Fridays are meant for relaxing. Winding down before
the business of the weekend.'

She shrugged and made no comment.

'I'll see you on Monday,' she said, facing him.

'I'll get the lift down with you.'

They walked together to the lift and as the doors shut he
turned to her and said, 'Big plans for tonight?'

'Not big, no. And you?' His eyes were boring into her
but she refused to look at him.

'Small plans, then?'

She clicked her tongue with impatience. There had been
no more prying into her personal life, not since that unset-
tling meal out three weeks previously, but for some reason
he was in the mood to stir and she was handy.

'I shall put my feet up and relax.'

'Isn't that what you did last Friday?' he mused thoughtfully, and she clenched her fists tightly around the handle
of her briefcase.

'Is it?' she asked innocently, refusing to become bait for
his sense of humour. 'I forget. I'm surprised you remember,
actually.'

'Oh, I remember everything. It's one of my talents.'

'Along with your modesty.'

He laughed under his breath. 'I hope we aren't working

you too hard...' His voice was speculative, paternal and didn't fool her for an instant. 'I wouldn't want to be accused of coming between you and your love life.'

The doors pinged open, and Jessica breathed a sigh of relief. Bruno was tenacious. When he got hold of something, he was like a dog with a bone, which was fine when it came to work, but when he started directing it at her private life she had an instinctive urge to dive and take cover.

'I'll make sure not to accuse you of any such thing, in that case,' she answered politely. They walked out of the building and into dark, driving rain.

'Have a good weekend.' He strolled off in the direction of the company's underground car park, and five minutes later she saw him sweep away, his car sending up a fine spray.

Jessica held her briefcase awkwardly over her head, ventured to the side of the kerb and waited for a vacant cab which, after fifteen minutes, was beginning to resemble a hunt for the proverbial needle in the haystack.

She should have walked to the underground, but her feet ached, and now it seemed pointless.

She was on the point of returning to the office and calling a taxi when a low-slung, sleek car slowed down and finally stopped in front of her. The window purred down and Bruno contemplated her wet, shivering form with a grin.

'Friday nights can be a bit difficult, especially wet Friday nights. Care for a lift?'

There was no possible excuse she could come up with this time. She could hardly tell him that she was having a grand time right where she was, huddled under her briefcase in a futile attempt not to become absolutely soaked to the skin.

He clicked open the passenger door and she hurried

round to the side, cursing fate, the weather and her idiocy in not walking to the underground, whatever the pathetic state of her aching feet.

'Thanks,' she said, slamming the door behind her. 'Filthy night. I'm afraid I'm dripping all over your seat.' She was feeling more bedraggled by the minute.

'I'm sure the car will recover from the shock of it,' he said gravely. 'Where to?'

She gave him her address, and leaned back, closing her eyes.

'What were you doing back at the office anyway?' she asked, easing her feet out of her shoes but not kicking them off completely.

'Oh, just some work I had to collect.'

'But...' She turned to look at his profile. 'Did you get what you returned for?'

'No. I saw your wet, forlorn shape and decided to do my good deed for the week instead.'

'How considerate.' As fast as the windscreen wipers cleared the screen, it became blurred with more running water.

'That's the sort of person that I am.'

He seemed, she thought, in a remarkably good mood considering he had found himself having to drive miles out of his way to deliver her to her house.

'I hope,' she said suddenly, 'I'm not ruining your plans for the evening.'

'Not at all. Don't give that another thought. I'd planned on spending the night in, actually.' He paused. 'Painting my nails and washing my hair.'

In the darkness, Jessica grinned. She had never known a man who could switch from aggressive to funny with such ease. In fact, she had never known a man whose personality was so complex. He could be ruthless, single-minded, persistent, utterly exasperating and madly, unbearably sarcastic. He could also be charming, witty and disconcertingly easygoing. Perhaps he had a split personality.

'Carry on along this road until you come to the next junction, then turn left.'

'How's your sister-in-law's baby?' he asked, after a few minutes' silence.

'My sister-in-law's baby?'

'The one she was due to have on the very day you couldn't possibly accept a lift home with me because you had to get back for a telephone call from your mother.'

'Oh. That sister-in-law. That baby.' That convoluted excuse. 'Both well and doing fine.' She had had the baby three days later, so as far as lies went that one was pretty close to the truth.

'Must be glad to have your mother out there to help,' he said casually, and Jessica didn't reply. She was not a revealing person by nature, and she seldom, if ever, discussed her family with anyone. Her background and all the attendant heartache was something she kept to herself.

'Guess so.'

'How long has your mother been over there? Seems a very far-flung place to go and live.'

'My brother was out there,' she said shortly, staring out of the window. Through the rain and the darkness, the lights looked like watery splashes of colour against a black, velvet background.

'But you were over here,' he pointed out, and she didn't say anything.

'I take it your silence means that I'm treading on delicate ground.'

'You're treading on ground that's none of your business,' she told him bluntly. 'Go straight over the traffic lights and my street's the third turning on the right.'

'How does your father fit into all this?'

Her fists curled into tight balls and she felt a knot of acid bitterness gather in her stomach. She had so successfully managed to slot her father into a disused cupboard in her mind that every time his memory was pulled out and dusted down, for whatever reason, she was overcome with the same, familiar feelings of anger.

'He died seven years ago,' she said tightly.

There must have been some indication of how she felt in her voice, because he glanced swiftly at her before turning back to the road.

'Should I offer you my sympathies?'

'You can offer whatever you care to.' Her father had spent his years ruling his house with a reign of terror, bellowing at her and her brother, lashing out at whoever had happened to be closest if his mood had happened to be off-key. Sympathy was the least appropriate feeling she could be offered, but there was no way that she would tell any of that to the man sitting next to her behind the steering wheel.

'My house is the third on the right. Bit hard to see in this weather, but you can just drop me off here.'

He slowed the car down and as she turned to face him, ready with her neat phrases of thanks and hope-it-wasn't-too-much-of-a-bother, he said, killing the engine and resting his head against the window, 'A cup of coffee would be nice. These are hellish conditions to be driving in.' He rubbed his eyes with his thumbs and she felt a pull of sympathy. He had been under no obligation to pick her up and drop her at her house, and whatever he had said about having no plans for that evening she was pretty certain that he had had. He was not a man to enjoy the comforts of a solitary meal, a cup of cocoa and a late-night movie, on a Friday night.

'Sure.' She got out of the car, only realising how thoroughly she had been drenched when the weight of her coat threatened to drag her to the ground. Her hair was still damp as well. She would look like a scarecrow in the morning.

'And perhaps you could rustle up something for us to eat,' he suggested, following her to the front door, then into the house.

In winter, she always made sure that she left the hall light on, so that when she returned home the place wasn't in complete darkness. And the heating had switched itself on three hours previously, so that it was beautifully warm inside. She felt some of the chill drain out of her bones.

'Rustle you up something to eat?' she asked, removing her coat and jacket and looking at him with incredulity.

'Nothing fancy. Just whatever you were going to do for yourself.' He was looking around without making it glaringly obvious, and he followed her into the small sitting room, with the large bay window overlooking the street. It was her favourite room in the house, the one she spent most of her time in, and had been decorated in warm, rich colours—deep greens and terracottas—and she had replaced the sixties-style electric fire with a real one, seldom used but beautiful to look at.

He strolled around it, dwarfing it in a way no one ever had before, looking at the photos of her mother and her brother with his family in their carefully chosen wood and silver frames. Did he notice that pictures of her father were conspicuously absent?

'I think it might be a good idea if you change,' he said out of the blue, turning to look at her, and she flushed. Yes, that had occurred to her but, no, she had had no intention of doing any such thing. Her working garb, however damp and bedraggled, was, somehow, her protection.

'Do you ever stop giving orders?' she asked politely.

'It's a bad habit of mine. You'll catch your death of cold if you stay like that.'

Jessica glared and watched as he removed his jacket, tossed it on to one of the chairs and sat down, stretching out his long legs in front of him.

'I won't be a minute,' she muttered.

Never mind bad habits, she thought, the man had some insufferable traits. She shut the bedroom door behind her, hesitating briefly, then locking it, though why she had no idea, and she stepped out of her shoes with a sigh of relief. Then she hurriedly flung on a white tee shirt and a pair of jeans, and replaced her shoes with the pair of worn, flat-heeled sandals she wore around the house.

She glanced at her reflection in the mirror and then un-pinned her hair, which had optimistically started the day as a perfectly coiled chignon. With speed born of habit, she plaited it, one long, blonde plait. Not exactly a sophisticated hairdo, she thought, but it would have to do.

When she returned, it was to hear rummaging in the kitchen, and she found him there with two wineglasses in his hand.

'I see you had some wine in your fridge.'

'Go right ahead and make yourself at home.'

'Care for a glass?' The bottle was on the kitchen table and, with a huge sigh of resignation, she nodded and he poured them both a glass.

'I really wouldn't want to keep you from whatever you had planned,' she began, folding her arms, uncomfortably aware that despite his casual attitude he had taken in her change of clothes, her alteration from businesswoman to homebody.

'Your hair is much longer than I thought.'

He had noticed *her hair?* What else had he noticed?

'There's not much to eat here. I'm not accustomed to cooking for someone else without preparation.'

'You wouldn't be trying to get rid of me, by any chance?' he asked, sitting on one of the chairs by the table and looking at her. There was amused challenge in his blue eyes and she went pink.

Was he a mind-reader or was she just a lot more obvious than she thought?

And what would he think if she admitted that she felt uncomfortable being in her house with him? She knew what he would think. He would think that he made her nervous, he would think that she felt more than merely the polite indifference of employee towards employer, which she had been at such pains to cultivate over the past few weeks. He would think that she was attracted to him.

She should have laughed at this conclusion, but instead of laughing to herself she felt a sudden surge of alarm.

'Of course I'm not trying to get rid of you!' she denied, her voice high. 'I just can't believe that you haven't got something more interesting to do on a Friday night than sit here and have a dreary meal with one of your employees.' It seemed a good idea to remind him that he was her boss.

'Between Rachels at the moment,' he said, and she could hear laughter in his voice.

So he was temporarily lacking in female companionship. That would account for the fact that some of that unused charm was spilling over onto her. He probably couldn't help himself. Under normal circumstances, she would be the last woman in the world he would look at twice, but they had been working closely together for a few weeks, albeit not always in perfect harmony, and he was without the distraction of a mistress.

'Poor old you,' she gushed with overdone sympathy. 'Your brain must be missing the intellectual stimulation.'

She paused, and then added, grudgingly, 'I apologise, that was uncalled for. She seemed a perfectly nice girl.' When in the company of men, she thought to herself.

'Oh, I think I'm doing all right on that front at the moment.' He tilted his glass towards her with a mocking salute, and she turned around and began foraging through the cupboards in search of something palatable for them to eat.

Her dietary requirements were virtually non-existent. Living on her own, she ate when she felt like it and very rarely cooked for herself. Pre-packaged foods were the norm, or else fresh bread and cheese. Sometimes, when she was particularly tired or particularly lazy, a bowl of cereal filled the gap.

She located a can of tuna and some tinned sweetcorn and then scoured the fridge for whatever else might be lurking there. Three tomatoes, she found, a bag of mushrooms which she had planned on using two days previously and half a tub of cream, which she surreptitiously sniffed just in case.

Clearing out her fridge on a daily basis was always one of her New Year's resolutions, and thus far never one that she had actually got around to putting into practice.

'Would you like a hand?' he asked from behind her and she shook her head.

'No. But I feel I should warn you that cooking was never one of my strong points, so don't expect anything exquisite.' She glanced over her shoulder to see him wearing that amused grin of his, the sort of grin that implied that her discomfort was a never-ending source of enjoyment to him.

'Oh, don't apologise. Lack of culinary skills is a trait I thoroughly approve of in a woman.'

'Strange. I thought that the way to a man's heart was through his stomach.' It was all right having this conversation with him while her back was turned away and while she could busy herself with the frying of mushrooms and tuna and all the ingredients that seemed to be converging into a colourful mishmash of food. Lord only knew what it would taste like. Whenever she cooked for someone else, she always made sure that a recipe book was close to hand. Spontaneous creations were things she tried to avoid at all costs.

'My point exactly.'

Jessica risked a look at him from over her shoulder, to gauge whether he was joking, but his expression was serious.

'Am I supposed to ask you to clarify?'

'I would have thought that I was being fairly obvious.'

'In other words, the way to your heart is firmly blocked off with a "No Trespassing" sign.'

Actually, she didn't need him to spell that out for her. One look at him was enough to tell her that he was a man who preferred the freedom to do precisely what he pleased without the obstruction of a wife. He worked long hours, was away for long stretches of time on business. In between, she assumed, he liked simple, undemanding recreation with someone who didn't tire him by challenging his intellect.

Her voice was light when she spoke. She stirred the contents of the saucepan, hoping that her mysterious, thrown-together concoction would not taste too appalling, and when she gauged that it was nearly cooked she put a pot of water to boil for some pasta. Then she sat down at the kitchen table and took a sip from her glass of wine.

She idly wondered what he would look like in jeans and a tee shirt. He had the sort of physique that was designed to look good in clothes. Wide shoulders, lean hips, long, muscular legs. Her heart began to beat a little faster.

'Was that Rachel's downfall?' she asked curiously. It occurred to her that this was hardly a typical boss-employee kind of conversation. She had had many amiable chats with Robert, her immediate boss, about his family, his grandchildren, his holiday plans. None of them had carried this intangible air of treading on delicate ground. She could feel herself stepping too close to quicksand, but when she looked a bit harder, to see if she could recognise the danger, there was nothing there.

He had given her a lift home because of the weather. She had invited him inside through politeness. She was now cooking him a meal out of guilt at having spoilt his evening. Where was the danger in that?

And if they weren't consumed with work talk, then what was the problem there? It was hardly as though she feared that he might suddenly draw a deep breath and lunge for her.

'I enjoy the family life,' he said with a careless shrug, 'just so long as it belongs to someone else.'

Jessica didn't answer. She tossed some pasta into the boiling water and then remained where she was with the glass in her hand, leaning against the kitchen counter.

She could understand what he was saying. The companionship of married life was never something that had beckoned. Her friends had taken to making dark comments about shelf-life, and intimating that they would arrange a love life for her if she didn't want to do it herself, and she always laughed at their underhand persistence. She simply could not conceive what it would be like to be tied to the cooker, waiting on a man hand and foot. As her mother had done for so many years.

'How do you feel about the lawsuit?' she asked, changing the subject abruptly. She didn't like it when her mind started wandering down the road of men and marriage and families, even if her response was to deny their importance in her life.

'Isn't that a question I should be asking *you*?' he returned, helping himself to more wine and watching her lazily as she began moving around the kitchen, opening drawers, pulling out crockery and cutlery.

She could feel his blue eyes on her and it made her skin tingle. It was a new experience for her. Normally, she had no difficulty in treating men as her equals but now, for some reason, she was acutely aware of her body, her movements, her hair dangling against her back. Her tee shirt was baggy and unrevealing, but she could feel the weight of her breasts beneath it, she could feel her nipples pushing against the thin, silky bra. A thin film of perspiration broke out over her body and when she began setting the table she found that she was purposefully avoiding his gaze.

'I don't think we have a problem,' she said, draining the pasta and tipping the contents of the frying pan into a casserole dish. 'When do you think I'll be able to have a look at those drawings?' She put the pasta and the tuna on the table and indicated for him to help himself.

'Oh, haven't I mentioned? Ralph Jennings delivered them to me this afternoon. I've got them in my briefcase, as a matter of fact.'

'You have?' She paused and looked at him with surprise. 'You should have mentioned that sooner. We could have gone over them at work.'

'You can have a look after we've eaten.' He began helping himself and she looked at him with sudden dismay.

Inexplicably, she didn't want him hanging around after dinner. She had anticipated feeding him and sending him on his way in the minimum amount of time.

'You haven't got a problem with that, have you?' he

asked, glancing up to catch her eye, and she shook her head hurriedly.

'No. I just feel a little...tired... I'm not sure I'll be able to concentrate fully...'

'It's a drawing,' he pointed out dryly. 'Fairly self-explanatory. It'll take ten minutes for me to run through it with you.'

'Yes. Fine,' she said dubiously, sitting down.

'Good. And don't worry about the concentration aspect. Even at half tilt, your brain is better than a lot of men's I've come across in my business dealings.'

'Thank you very much for the compliment.' She was certain that there had been a time when she would have been thrilled at what he had just said, but now she had a hollow feeling of disappointment. She supposed that it was akin to being described as 'one of the lads'. Was that *ever* a compliment for a woman? Who wanted to be 'one of the lads'?

For the first time ever, she wondered what it would be like to be remarked upon for her looks as opposed to her brains. Her boyfriends had always appreciated her intelligence, had warmed to the fact that she had definite opinions on most things, and she had never found that a matter for complaint.

Now, she thought, What would it be like to be a Rachel? Blonde and fluffy and undemanding, with bedroom eyes and a smile that promised sex?

Ridiculous notion, she told herself shakily.

But now that the thought had taken root, it began eating away inside her, nibbling insidiously at all her firmly held beliefs that intelligence in a woman was what mattered, that men who were attracted to the outside packaging were not the sort of men she could ever be interested in.

She heard his voice wash over her as he discussed intri-

cacies of the lawsuit, and she knew that she was responding
with all the correct answers, but it was as if she was suddenly functioning on autopilot, while her brain wandered
along its merry way.

She was not an unattractive woman. She knew that. True,
she might not be overtly sexy in the way that the Rachels
of this world were, but neither was she a picture of plain-
ness. Her problem, she realised, was her inability to play
up her good points. Her figure was quite acceptable, but
she never wore tight clothes. Her long, well-shaped legs
were always hidden under calf-length skirts or trousers. Her
hair, thick and long and naturally blonde, was always
pinned back severely into her neck. Her approach was essential in her career, but it hardly turned heads, did it?

Just thinking like this flustered her, and she couldn't wait
for the meal to finish, hastily rejecting his offer to help with
the washing-up, rambling on about doing it herself after he
had gone because she found it strangely relaxing. Good
heavens. Washing dishes was something she found
strangely tedious, but the thought of standing next to him
at a kitchen sink and doing a mundane domestic chore was
almost beyond her level of tolerance.

'What about the drawings?' he asked, after she had
cleared the table and positioned herself by the kitchen door
in readiness for his departure. He stood up, stretched
slightly, and she dragged her eyes away from him.

'In the sitting room, I guess,' she said brightly, with a
sinking heart. She had forgotten the wretched drawings.

They walked through to the sitting room, where the light-
ing seemed mellow and intimate after the fluorescent glare
of the overhead kitchen lights, and she sat down on the
edge of the sofa and waited as he pulled some papers out
of his briefcase.

Then he sat next to her and spread the drawings out on

the low, square coffee-table in front of them. His weight had depressed the sofa. She could feel her thigh lightly touching his and she did her utmost to ignore the sensation. She peered obligingly at the various angles he was pointing out to her, and she nodded and made all the right noises under her breath, but her eyes were mesmerised by his long fingers, and against her his thigh was scorching through her jeans, making all her nerve-endings come alive.

'These are the originals,' he said, inclining very slightly to look at her, and their eyes tangled, brown with blue. Their faces were so close that she could see the fine lines around his eyes, could appreciate the dark thickness of his eyelashes. Could eyelashes be sultry? There was something sultry about his eyelashes. 'Naturally, I shall get copies for the court appearance next week.'

'Naturally,' Jessica said faintly.

'If you want to hang on to these for the weekend...? Have a look at them?' He was looking at his watch, standing up, and she wondered whether he had had enough of her company now. The novelty of conversing with an intelligent woman was wearing off. It was time for him to be on his way. His mind was already striding ahead, planning the rest of his weekend. Was there a replacement Rachel hovering somewhere in the wings? Probably.

'Yes, that would be helpful.' She levered herself off the couch and plastered a bland but wide smile on her face. 'Now, I think my work with you is pretty much finished,' she said, holding on to the smile with difficulty, but loath to let go of it because she had no idea what it would be replaced by. 'So next week I shall take up permanent residence once again at my own office.' She walked him to the door, arms folded.

'And take over where Robert left off.' He turned to her

with a smile. 'Whatever the outcome, you appear to have done a thorough job on this damned lawsuit.'

'As thorough as any man?'

He raised one eyebrow expressively. 'Is that a hint that you want an apology from me?'

'I wouldn't be so mad,' she said wryly, and in the awkward intervening few seconds, as she wondered what next to say, he solved the dilemma by holding out his hand.

'Good work, Miss Stearn. You have the job.' He grinned as he shook her hand, then he was gone. Out of the door, into his car and away into the night.

On a handshake.

She shut the door reflectively behind her and the last thing to go through her head that night was the foggy image of his mouth on hers, his hands exploring her body, his body against her. No handshake. Just something else.

with a smile. "Whatever the outcome, your presence have done a thorough job on this damned lawsuit."

"As thorough as my best."

He raised one eyebrow speculatively. "Is that a hint that you want an apology...?"

"I wouldn't go to cost," she said wryly, and in the awkward...

# CHAPTER FOUR

IT WAS in the newspapers. Bruno Carr, after all, was news. He might not be a movie star, Jessica reflected, or a TV personality, but he had the looks, the money and the charisma to grab headlines. The newspapers carried the same image—Bruno emerging from court with his name fully cleared.

Red-nosed, dosed up with paracetamol, and in bed, Jessica read the full commentary in the business section of the newspaper and then re-read it four times.

We did it! she thought. She might have been an important part in piecing together all the evidence, but it had taken a great deal of persistent hard slog, and she had no doubt that her four staff who had worked overtime and weekends to make sure that the case was wrapped up in the minimum amount of time were feeling as euphoric as she was. If a little less under the weather.

It was just a shame that she couldn't have been at the court to witness the victory herself.

She blew her nose into some tissues and flung them into the waste-paper basket which she had strategically placed next to the bed, and which was becoming progressively fuller.

Bruno Carr had swept into her life like a tornado, and now that her part had been played he would vanish without leaving a trace. She lay back on the pillows, closed her eyes and succumbed to feelings of maudlin self-pity.

It was this wretched bug, of course. That was why she felt so low. She had spent the weekend feeling vaguely washed out, and that had progressed onto the familiar aching bones, fever, runny nose and desire to keep the curtains tightly drawn. She hadn't had flu in years. Normally, she was as healthy as a horse.

'Your immune system's up the spout,' her friend Amy had informed her, when she had telephoned earlier in the week to cancel their dinner arrangement. 'You need to take a break.'

So here I am now, she thought glumly, taking a much-deserved break. Who in their right mind would choose to go for a week's vacation to somewhere hot, exotic and sunny when they could lie in bed, sneezing and running a fever instead? That was what standing in the driving, cold rain waiting for a non-existent taxi did for a girl.

She punched the pillows, buried her head in them with a stifled groan, and was debating whether she should bother to leave the bed at all for the rest of the day when the doorbell went.

Through the pillows, it was a muffled noise, and Jessica muttered a venomous, 'Go away' to whoever had the nerve to call when she was indisposed.

The rings became less polite and more insistent, and she eventually dragged herself out of bed, slung on her dressing gown and padded across to the front door.

When she yanked it open and saw Bruno standing outside, his hand poised to press the bell again, she scowled ferociously, aware of the less-than-stunning picture she presented with her runny, red nose and her hair flopping every which way as though it hadn't seen a comb in years.

'How are you feeling?' he asked, and her scowl deepened. It was eleven-thirty in the morning, she was still in her pyjamas and dressing gown, the kitchen was proudly sporting dishes that had not been washed for two days. It seemed a particularly stupid question. 'Everyone's very concerned about you. They seem to have been under the illusion that you have an in-built immunity to ill health.' He grinned slightly. 'Naturally I rushed over because if that's the case you're about to go down in medical history. There could be a fortune in it for you.'

'I feel the way I look,' she told him, pulling her robe tighter around her and reaching behind with one hand to try and get her hair into some sort of order. 'Congratulations, by the way. I read several versions of it in the newspapers.' She gave him a wry look. 'Not that it would take a genius to work out what the outcome had been. You'll have to be careful not to blind people with your high spirits.'

'Mind if I come in? It's freezing out here. Won't do your cold any good at all if you have to stand by an open door having a conversation with me.'

Come in? A social call? He stared at her, refusing to be willed away, until she eventually stood aside to let him in, then she shoved the door shut behind her.

'I'm not good with people when I'm ill,' she told his back as he headed in the direction of the sitting room, for all the world as though he belonged there. 'I'm snappy, short-tempered and I'd really rather just be left alone to get on with my recuperation.' She stood with her hands on her hips and watched as he removed his jacket, dropped it inelegantly on the coffee-table, and then settled into a chair.

'Yes, quite a victory.' He didn't pause to let her answer. 'As you couldn't make it to the court, I thought I'd drop by to congratulate you personally on the result.'

'I didn't do it on my own,' Jessica informed him, thawing slightly but still not enough to view his presence in the house with warmth. 'We all worked very hard to make sure that it got resolved as quickly as possible.'

'And I have congratulated them all myself.'

'Right. That's very good of you.' She paused and sneezed, fishing a tissue out of the pocket of her dressing gown.

'Have you been to a doctor?'

He wasn't going to oblige by vanishing through the front door. Jessica reluctantly sat down on the sofa and tucked her feet underneath her.

She would never have admitted it in a million years, but the thought of being seen by him in all her snuffling lack of glory was enough to make her cringe with self-consciousness. She had always maintained that the body was infinitely less important than the mind, but right now she would have given her right arm to at least have had the foresight to have changed into normal clothes earlier on. Instead of blearily thinking that it involved just too much effort.

'Doctors can't do anything for viruses,' she said. 'You just have to wait for them to take their course.'

'You look a wreck.'

'Oh, thank you very much,' Jessica replied, knowing that it was perfectly true, but nonetheless not caring for his observation. 'It did occur to me when I got up this morning that I should camouflage my red nose under six layers of cleverly applied make-up, but my eyes were watering too much for me to see what I was doing, and I gave up halfway through. 'Course, if I'd known that I was going to be bombarded with visitors, I might have persisted in my efforts.'

'Tut-tut. You certainly weren't kidding when you said that all good humour flew through the window the minute you got ill.'

'Did I say that?'

'Along those lines. Now, why don't you stay where you are and I'll go and fetch you a cup of tea?'

'That's very kind, but, really, there's no need. I appreciate your gesture in coming over here…' ha, ha '…but I'd really rather be on my own. And I'm sure you can think of better ways of celebrating your victory than sharing a room with me and thousands of contagious little germs….' She yawned, only remembered to put her hand over her mouth halfway through, and squashed herself into a more comfortable position on the sofa.

'Nonsense! You should have someone around here, though, to help out if you're ill. Is there no one who could come round and look after you?'

'I don't need looking after!' Jessica said, more sharply than she had intended. 'I'm perfectly capable of looking after myself.'

'I take it that means no.' He stood up, waving her back down when she attempted to follow suit, and she heard him as he headed to the kitchen, then the muffled noises of him making them a cup of tea.

Why had she become so defensive just then? He had asked a perfectly reasonable question and she had jumped down his throat, and the worst of it was she knew why. She had no one. Oh, she had a handful of friends. They went out and had a good time every so often, but there was no one who could come around and look after her if she ever needed looking after.

She was twenty-eight years old, successful in her career, owned her own house and could afford to go on holiday whenever she cared to, but what did all that count for when at the end of the day she had no one to share any of it with?

She couldn't remember thinking this way before. She had measured her worth as she'd climbed the steady ladder of success. She had watched as her friends had married, settled down, in a couple of cases had their first children, and she had never felt the stirrings of envy. She had been vaguely curious as to how their lifestyles would change, but she had held on to her own steady fortunes in the never-ending stormy waters of chance with a feeling of relief.

'Not everyone needs a caretaker,' she announced as Bruno walked back in with a mug of tea in his hand, and he looked at her questioningly.

'You've lost me.'

Jessica took a sip of hot tea, made a face, and then looked at him as he settled on the sofa, which meant that she now wouldn't be able to stretch out her legs if she wanted to.

'I can look after myself,' she told him. 'I don't want you to feel sorry for me.'

'I don't recall mentioning that I did.'

'You don't have to mention it. You can imply it without saying so in so many words.'

'Okay. If it makes you feel happier, I won't feel sorry for you.'

There he goes again, she thought with exasperation, patronising. He *did* feel sorry for her, and it had nothing to do with her temporary ill health. He felt sorry for her because he compared her to the women he knew, women who went out every night and owned a wardrobe full of designer outfits, women whose lives were never free of men, who skirted from one relationship to another without pause in between. She could feel it in the way he looked at her sometimes.

'Good,' she said, disgruntled.

'How are you eating?'

'With my teeth, like everyone else.' His concern, for some reason, was catapulting her into another bout of self-pity. When was the last time anyone had brought her a cup of tea? she thought, on the verge of tears at this point.

'I see your cold hasn't done away with that viper tongue of yours.' His mouth twitched, and she steadfastly refused to look at him. She cradled the mug in her hands, feeling the warm, rough texture under her fingers. It was vaguely soothing.

'Have you eaten?' he asked bluntly.

'Why? Are you about to offer your talents as in-house chef?' The man was simply trying to be pleasant, but for some reason she found it hard to stomach. She wished he had stuck to the brief he had initially presented to her—of a man who was ruthless, self-assured, autocratic and took pains to hide none of those qualities. She couldn't cope with his wit, his sense of humour and, worst, his attempts to be considerate.

'Look,' he said, standing up, 'I'm beginning to wish that I hadn't bothered to drop by. If you'd rather lie and wallow in your misery, then far be it from me to disturb you.' He reached down for his jacket, and Jessica took a deep breath.

'I...' she struggled, looking at her fingers. 'I...I'm...'

'I haven't got all day. Spit it out.'

Wasn't that more like it? He damned well knew what she wanted to say, but he was going to make sure that he didn't let her off the hook.

'I'm sorry if I appeared rude.'

'You didn't *appear* rude. You *were* rude.'

Jessica blushed. 'Okay. I apologise.' This seemed insufficient. He still had his jacket in his hand, and she now realised that she desperately did not want him to leave. She didn't want her final impression on him to be of an ill-mannered, surly, belligerent woman who had neither the good grace nor common courtesy to express her thanks to someone who had paid her a visit out of kindness. Much as she loathed the thought of being seen as a charity case, which was what his kindness implied.

'I'm so accustomed to my independence that I don't deal very well when my body lets me down. I have a pile of work waiting for me at the office, and I simply cannot afford to take time off to be ill.'

'The place won't self-destruct because you're out of it for a few days.' He sighed, and she eyed him surreptitiously as he dumped the jacket back on the coffee-table and looked at her. 'So have you eaten? A simple yes or no answer will do.'

'Not much,' Jessica admitted reluctantly.

'I'll make you something.'

Before she could object, he sauntered off and she lay back and closed her eyes. She wouldn't swap her lifestyle for any of her married friends' lifestyles, of course she wouldn't, but for a minute she conceded that there might be one or two advantages to the married life. One of them had to be a husband who fetched cups of tea when necessary. None of her previous boyfriends had ever come near to fitting any such role, and Bruno Carr, despite the fact that he could bring a grin to her lips at the least expected moments, was definitely not the sort of man who could ever be a contender, but... She imagined someone thoughtful, caring, kind, good background and a dab hand at cooking. Might not be too bad after all.

She was nodding off when Bruno said from over her, 'Wake up, Sleeping Beauty. Feeding time.'

Jessica rubbed her eyes and sat up, swinging her legs over the side of the sofa to accommodate the tray he was carrying.

'Nothing very fancy, I'm afraid.'

He set the tray on her lap, and her mouth watered at the sight of two slices of toast smothered in creamy scrambled egg. Much better than anything she could have produced herself, but then scrambled eggs had always been a problem for her.

'Thank you very much,' she said, tucking into the food, and only realising the depth of her hunger when she bit into the toast and egg. She had eaten nothing for the past day and a half. 'Tastes delicious.'

'Things have a tendency to, when someone else does the cooking.' He perched on the coffee-table and regarded her.

'You do this often, do you?' she asked absent-mindedly, concentrating on feeding her hunger as rapidly as she could without appearing utterly inelegant in the process.

'I think this is a first for me,' he told her dryly, and she shot him a quick, surprised look.

'Clever of you to avoid going out with women who catch the occasional cold,' she said mildly. 'Or do you just avoid them when they're careless enough to get ill?'

'Care to fill me in on precisely what you're saying?'

'I'm not saying anything.' She ducked her head and concentrated on eating.

'Oh, yes, you are. I've noticed something about you. You're good at initiating criticism, in that cowardly, back-handed fashion of yours, but you don't like it if it's pursued, do you? You're not up to defending anything you say.'

'It wasn't meant to be a criticism,' Jessica mumbled, mortified at what he had said, which was perfectly true. 'It was just an observation.'

'I don't make it a habit of cooking for women, any more than I make it a habit of having women cook for me.'

'Should I consider myself flattered, in that case?' She asked the question without thinking about it, but when she looked at him his eyes were cool and speculative.

'You can consider it anything you want to. As far as I'm concerned, it just means that you're not my woman.'

He let the words sink in, in all their brutal simplicity. She was his employee, and that was the full extent of it. Beyond that, she meant nothing at all to him, and so whether she made him a meal, or he cooked her some eggs, was irrelevant. Theirs was not a relationship and so was not threatening.

'But that's not why I came here. I came here to congratulate you on the court case, and found you ill and clearly incapable of looking after yourself...'

'I am perfectly capable of looking after myself!' Jessica retorted indignantly.

'So you've told me. Is that why you looked as though you hadn't eaten for a week?'

'I didn't get around to it...' she returned, feeling more and more like a charity case, and hating it.

'So I made you something to eat.' He shrugged and stood up.

Does he think that I'm trying to attach significance to that? she wondered, with a growing sense of shame. Did he think that she was after him, looking for ways of misinterpreting simple actions into something meaningful?

Yes. Of course he thought that. She could feel herself getting hot and flustered and horribly embarrassed.

He was the archetypal eligible bachelor. She suspected that he would have spent his entire adult life being pursued by women. It would hardly surprise him if he thought that she had joined the queue. She cringed inwardly. Good Lord, he was warning her off him!

'Yes, I know. I know, I know, I know. I'm being a bore. It's this inactivity. I hate it. I need to be *doing*.' She transferred tray from lap to table.

'Makes you feel like a worthwhile member of society, does it?'

Jessica closed her eyes and rested her head against the

back of the sofa. 'Something like that. Either that or I'm an undiagnosed hyperactive and in desperate need of medication.'

'You should try slowing down now and again.'

She half opened her eyes and looked at him. 'Do you?'

'No, but I'm a man.' He waited for her expression to change and then burst out laughing. 'Works a treat every time! Now you have a steaming cold to contend with and high blood pressure from trying to stifle your little flare of self-righteous anger at my remark, but at least the wallowing inclination's disappeared for the moment. Now, doctor's orders: I shouldn't bother coming into work for the rest of the week.' He eyed her up and down in the manner of a scientist sizing up a particularly stubborn strain of bacteria.

'I'll see how it goes,' Jessica said vaguely, not caring for his jovial brand of high humour. Of all the things he made her feel, feminine was not in the list and she wondered whether it was his deliberate ploy to remind her that any concern for her was purely altruistic.

She remembered Rachel, with the flaxen hair and babydoll look; Rachel who had made the mistake of becoming a little too clingy and therefore had had to be dispensed with. Did he imagine that she might have seen his small act of kindness as encouragement?

She began standing up and he waved her down.

'Actually, I haven't quite said what I came to say,' he informed her, slinging on his jacket.

'Which is?'

'You and your team have done a fine job, and I want to recognise that.'

'I'm sure it's enough for you to tell them that personally,' Jessica said, omitting to mention that a bonus would probably do the trick even more.

'Which is why,' he carried on, ignoring her input, 'I wanted to ask your advice.'

'*My* advice? Where's my diary? I should make a note of this red-letter day.'

'I'll put that remark down to ill health.' He gave her another wolfish grin. 'You know your team far better than I do.'

'True.' She nodded sagely, then, unable to resist the temptation, added, 'They really don't see much of you, considering you *are* their boss.'

He frowned, and she smiled placidly at him.

'I thought a weekend away might be a nice idea...'

'A weekend away? Where?' She hoped he wouldn't suggest a health farm. She couldn't think of a single member of her staff who would appreciate a weekend at a health farm. They were all far too young to see the advantages of a place that offered only nutritional food on their menu and a complete absence of alcohol.

'Somewhere hot, I think, don't you?'

They both automatically looked in the direction of the bay window, through which leaden skies promised the worst of English weather.

'I'm sure they would be thrilled,' Jessica said, with genuine sincerity. 'This weather's awful, isn't it?'

'Grim.'

'When did you have in mind?'

'This weekend, actually. If the office could do without manning for a couple of days.'

'*This weekend?*' The man obviously had no touch with reality if he thought that tickets to anywhere in the Med could be bought at such short notice. 'And of course the office would be manned. Why shouldn't it be?'

'By whom?'

'Well, me for a start, and then there are the secretaries

and all the other people who have had nothing to do with the lawsuit…'

'Fourteen in all, including yourself.'

'You want to take the entire office on a weekend to somewhere hot?' She gave an incredulous laugh.

'What are your objections?'

'Oh, none at all!' Jessica informed him airily. 'Of course, the airlines might have a few. I doubt any of them could fly thirteen people over to sunny Spain at a moment's notice!'

'Whoever mentioned sunny Spain? Which, incidentally, wouldn't be all that sunny at this time of the year. And what do airlines have to do with anything?'

'Well, how else would you suggest they travel?' she asked, with a hint of saccharine sarcasm in her voice. 'Swim?'

'I own a small private jet.'

'You…own…a…private…jet… Of course, don't we all? What household is complete without one?'

'I also own an island in the Caribbean,' he drawled.

'*You own an island in the Caribbean?*' She stared at him, open-mouthed.

'Of course. Don't we all? What household is complete without one?'

Jessica went pink. Why was it that her mouth seemed to develop a will of its own the minute this man was around?

'So you're planning on whisking my entire office off to your private island, in your private jet, for a long weekend.'

'That's about the size of it. Do you think that they would appreciate the gesture?'

'Appreciate might be understating their reaction.' She thought that they might just keel over from shock, and one or two of the older ones, Mary and Elizabeth, in their fifties, might well have to be resuscitated.

'And what about you?'

'What about me?'

'You're included in the list of invitees. I take it you'll be over your cold by Friday?'

She didn't want to go. Private jets to private islands with Bruno Carr lurking in the background somewhere were not her idea of a relaxing time.

'I'm not sure that it'll be possible for me to come as well.'

'Why not?'

'Because…I've already missed enough work, what with having to do so much on this court case. I need to get back to the office and catch up with what's been going on.'

'It can wait a few more days.'

She fidgeted in silence for a while, unable to pinpoint why she felt so apprehensive at a free weekend break in the sun.

'When was the last time you had a holiday?' he asked lazily, and she frowned and thought about the question.

'Some time ago,' she finally admitted. 'My lifestyle doesn't seem to accommodate holidays.'

'Your lifestyle doesn't seem to accommodate holidays?' She heard the irony in his voice and flinched.

'I'm a very busy woman,' she told him stiffly. 'I haven't got the time to go gallivanting around the world at a moment's notice.' What she found she meant was that the years seemed to have rushed by. She had been so wrapped up in her exams, then in her jobs, proving her worth, working all out so that she could stake her claim for financial independence, that she had barely noticed the passing of time. It had been five years since she'd had anything resembling a real holiday. Yes, she had had the occasional long weekend, and a few days off around Christmas, but a fortnight relaxing somewhere, far away from the madding crowd, was a luxury she had almost forgotten existed.

'Of course, it's a very generous offer...'

'Isn't it?' he said coolly. 'But not one you feel you can accept...'

'If I hadn't had these past couple of days off work, ill...'

'In that case, I'm sure you won't mind breaking the news to the rest of your staff that you rejected my offer on their behalf. I'm sure they'll understand.'

He turned around and was heading towards the door, and she scrambled after him.

'What do you mean? Are you telling me that if I don't come, then the bonus break's off for everyone else?'

He stopped abruptly and swung round to face her, so that she very nearly catapulted into his chest.

'Got it in one.'

'That's not fair!'

'Why not? I won't be there for the first day or so, if at all. I need the security of knowing that there'll be someone loosely in charge.'

'They're all adults!'

'Your choice.' He shrugged and looked at her, and eventually she sighed.

'Okay. I'll go. I should be fine by then.' Besides, if Bruno Carr wasn't going to be there, then she would be able to relax, and she needed a rest. Her body was telling her so.

'My secretary will contact you with all the details by Thursday afternoon.'

He rested his hand on the door handle, and then said, in passing, 'It's gratifying to know that you *are* capable of thinking of someone other than yourself.'

'And what is *that* supposed to mean?' she demanded as he opened the door and began heading towards his car.

He didn't bother to turn around. He just called out, in the voice of someone utterly indifferent to what she might or might not think of his remark, 'Why don't you take to your bed and think about it?'

Then he was gone, leaving her speechless with indignation. Yet again.

# CHAPTER FIVE

BRUNO CARR was beginning to occupy quite a bit of space in Jessica's head. But he wouldn't be around and the change in weather would do her good.

She kept those two things uppermost in her mind as she boarded the private jet on the Friday.

It was cold and blustery, and, not quite knowing what the temperatures would be when they landed, she had bundled herself up in jeans, a tee shirt, long-sleeved shirt and thick jumper.

Not everyone in the team of eleven was quite so restrained. Ronnie, the youngest of the secretaries, had braved the British elements in a short, flimsy skirt, which blew around her as she climbed the metal staircase, causing great jollity amongst the six young men behind her, and at the top of the stairs she posed, giggling, in an imitation of Marilyn Monroe until Jessica called dryly for her to get in before she caught her death of cold.

'I'm so excited,' she confided to Jessica as they buckled in. 'I've never been abroad before.'

'Never?' Jessica asked incredulously. True, Ronnie was only eighteen, but she was still surprised that there were people left who had not had a holiday abroad at some point in their lives.

'My dad hates flying,' she explained in a high, breathless voice, peering out of the window even though the view was nothing more impressive than the runway, barely visible in the darkness. 'So we always took our holidays in England.'

'What happened to the rest of the skirt, Ron?' one of the

men asked, pausing to grin at the blonde teenager, and she stuck her tongue out. 'Did it go on holiday ahead of you?' General guffaws all round, and Jessica rested her head back and closed her eyes with a smile.

Thank goodness she had made the effort. She would never have been forgiven by her staff if she had squashed the idea flat.

The bonus, when it had been put to them, had been met with uncontainable enthusiasm. Even Mary and Elizabeth, after tut-tutting about short notice and wondering what their respective husbands would do for supper, had greeted the scheme with delight.

They all needed a rest. They had worked hard over the past few weeks, and they deserved a break. And, Jessica thought as the plane slowly began its ascent, as breaks went, they didn't really get more impressive.

Four days of tropical bliss. They wouldn't even need to think about cooking, because housekeepers would be there, taking care of the food, the cleaning and, from the sound of it, pretty much everything else.

She heard the excited chatter around her as the plane cut a path through the sky, and decided that this was going to do her the world of good after all.

Her flu was on the way out, but she still felt lethargic, and work would have been a strain had she gone back. It also occurred to her that it had been a very long time since she had relaxed totally. Over the past couple of years, her breaks had tended to involve decorating the house. Enjoyable enough, because she quite liked the mindless physical exertion of wallpapering and painting walls, but she would hardly describe it as flaking out.

Before that, she dimly recalled a disastrous week in Portugal with her boyfriend at the time. After only nine months of going out, it had been a last-ditch attempt to

energise their love life. Instead, he had fallen head over
heels in love with a girl on holiday from Manchester, and
Jessica had spent the week sunbathing on her own and listening patiently to his attempts at apology.

Holidays had always made her apprehensive. She could
remember going on holiday with her parents, fearfully trying to have a good time with her brother in an atmosphere
of frozen politeness, waiting for her father to do something
to break the temporary cease-fire.

This short break would be different. She was not expected by anyone to have a good time. She could do precisely as she pleased. Lie on the beach with a book, or else
doze with her hat over her face, and let time sweep past
her, for once. She had brought a couple of novels with her,
making sure to leave behind any law books.

The background noise of the engines eventually lulled
her into a kind of sleep, and she was roused when they
were told to fasten their seat belts in preparation for land-
ing.

Then she sat up, and peered curiously through the small
window as a small island took shape. There seemed to be
nothing to it. A dot of land in the middle of sea. There
were some lights to indicate the landing-strip, but the darkness prevented her from making out any details, and she
settled back as the plane bumped along the ground and
finally screeched to a stop.

There was a chorus of voices as everyone reached for
their bags, and Ronnie said, grinning, 'I can't believe we're
here!' Her blue eyes gleamed. 'Can you believe Mr Carr—
oops, Bruno—*actually owns an island*?'

'Amazing, isn't it?' Jessica said, half smiling and half
yawning, as she stood up. 'The lengths some people will
go to to guarantee a bit of privacy for themselves.'

'I don't even have privacy in the bathroom at home,'

Ronnie was saying cheerfully to her as she yanked out her enormous holdall from underneath the seat in front. 'You wouldn't believe how long teenage boys spend preening themselves!'

'I can imagine!' Jessica returned with a laugh. Her father had been a stickler for timekeeping. She and Jeremy had never seen the bathroom as somewhere to indulge. There had been no preening in front of the bathroom mirror, or reading a book in the bath. Life had always been too disciplined for such indulgences. Most of all, mess had been unacceptable. Every morning, before school, her father would push open the bathroom door and check that everything was spick and span, or else there would be hell to pay, and such lessons were to be avoided at all costs.

Outside, there were two Jeeps waiting for them, but the very first thing they all noticed was the incredible heat. Even at this hour of the night the air was warm, with a lazy breeze doing its best to keep the temperature down. Jumpers were pulled off and shoved over handles of holdalls, and Ronnie, with gleeful satisfaction, raised both arms in the air and asked who was laughing at her outfit now. In her frothy short skirt and skimpy top, she was certainly the most sensibly dressed for the weather, albeit a bit on the overdressed side.

They climbed onto the Jeeps, chatting, and as they bumped along the makeshift road, through a forest of tall, swaying palm trees and bush, Jessica could feel the heat turning her jeans into rubber and her tee shirt into cling film. She hadn't travelled with much. One small case with the barest of essentials. A couple of tee shirts, some shorts, some swimsuits and a cardigan, *just in case,* although, feeling the heat, she had no idea what had possessed her to include this last item in the packing.

The house was a matter of a few minutes' drive away,

and it was already so late by the time they arrived that they were shown immediately to their rooms, none of which was shared.

Lord only knew how many rooms the place had. Jessica, her eyes heavy with exhaustion, vaguely noticed lots of wood everywhere: wooden floors, wooden ceilings, and a labyrinthine network of areas, leading to various different parts of the house.

Her room was large and airy with an overhead fan and a soft mosquito net draped over a double-sized bed. There were rugs on the floor and through an opened door she saw an *en suite* bathroom. It was all very luxurious, she thought, dumping her bag on a chair. The thought of having a shower was tempting, but the thought of changing into her pyjamas in under five seconds and flopping on the bed underneath the mosquito net was even more so.

She switched on the fan, felt obliged to peer through one of the large, veranda-style windows, then slipped on her striped pyjamas, and within ten minutes she was asleep.

When she next opened her eyes, it was to find sunlight streaming into the bedroom, and she groggily realised that it was after ten in the morning.

Through sheer habit, she felt her stomach go into knots at the thought of having overslept. It was something she rarely did, if ever. Her father had never allowed it, and her body had adapted to suit from a very early age.

When she pushed open the slatted wooden window, it was to be greeted with the most perfect sight she had ever seen in her life before. The house was on the beach. White sand and turquoise sea were visible through a latticework of palm trees.

She dressed quickly, flinging on a black bikini, then she grabbed her sun cream, a pair of shades, her hat, a book and rushed out of the house.

'About time you got up!' she heard Ronnie's voice from behind her, and she waved and laughed.

'Where's everyone?' she asked.

'Sunbathing, swimming, exploring! I'm back out in a couple of minutes. Can't waste this weather!'

'No. We might not see it again till summer rolls round in England. If it decides to!'

How on earth could a few hours on a plane make such a difference? She couldn't believe that she had devoted so much time to feeling guilty about work, imagining the mounds of it collecting in her in-tray with relentless, sneering persistence, thinking about how much of her weekends would be eaten up in trying to reduce the swelling pile. As she stepped onto the sand and felt it slipping warmly through her bare feet, work seemed like something vaguely unpleasant that was happening millions of light years away.

Mary and Elizabeth, paired off as usual, were further along the beach, two portly figures modestly attired in dark-coloured one-pieces and shaded with broad-brimmed straw hats. Further along, Ronnie's cronies were fooling around in the water.

Jessica waved and then found herself a more secluded part of the beach, under a palm tree, and she lay down on her towel and slowly plastered herself with sun cream.

The sound of the sea was lulling, a lazy, lapping noise as the water washed against the sand, ebbing away, with the steady in and out rhythm of something alive and breathing. She had brought her book with her, but the glare in her eyes was too strong to read comfortably, and after five minutes she gave in to the irresistible impulse to close her eyes and drift off. Sea, sun, sand, a cool breeze, tranquillity, and a deep, velvety voice in her right ear saying, 'You have to be careful, you know. With your complexion, there's a good chance you could end up looking like broiled lobster.'

Jessica's eyes flew open to confront Bruno Carr standing over her, with two cold drinks in his hands. The vision was so unexpected that she blinked a few times, convinced that the heat must have caused some dreadful mirage to appear. On the fifth blink, she realised that this was no mirage.

'What are you doing here?' she said, sitting up, desperately aware of how much of her body was exposed in her black bikini. Every nerve in her body seemed to have gone on red alert, and, although she did her best to keep her eyes plastered to his face, she was all too aware of his muscular body, more tanned than she would have expected, and clothed only in a short-sleeved cotton shirt, unbuttoned, and a pair of trunks.

Thank goodness for her sunglasses! At least they offered her some protection from the shock of seeing him here. And where was her hat? She grabbed it from next to her and stuck it on, so that her face was instantly half covered.

'Care for a drink?' He handed her a glass of something long and cold, and she took it from him quickly with a bright, 'Thanks.'

'What are you doing here?' she repeated, in a more normal voice. 'I thought you said that you weren't going to be coming.'

'Did I?' He looked at her with an expression of amazement. 'You must have misunderstood. I said that I might not be able to come over for the full time, but as you can see...' he sipped his drink, and, disturbingly because it threatened a longer stay than she wanted, sat down on the edge of her towel, so that she had to make a few imperceptible adjustments to further the distance between them '...I managed to make it over.'

'So I see,' Jessica mumbled.

'Call me a fool, but I couldn't resist the temptation of seeing you without your handy working-woman face on. Efficient cool lawyer by day, efficient cool lawyer by night—didn't make sense. So I rearranged my affairs to see if I could catch a rare glimpse of the only occasionally spotted Jessica Stearn—woman.' He chuckled, thoroughly amused at his wit, and she refused to indulge him by responding.

'Sometimes I wonder how you manage to be so successful,' she said tartly, 'when bird-spotting is such a great pastime of yours.'

'I don't think I said that. Quite.' He shot her a dark, outrageously flirtatious look and grinned. 'Only one species in particular.'

Unable to find a suitable response to that, Jessica resorted to a look of complete disdain, which made him grin even more.

'What do you think of it?'

'Fine. It's your house, after all.'

'No,' he said softly into her ear, which made her shift over a bit more in alarm, 'I meant what do you think of the place, not what do you think about my being here.'

'Oh.' She turned to look at him, and before she knew what was happening he reached out and removed her sunglasses in one neat movement.

'Could you please return those?' she asked, opening her hand.

'I dislike talking to people when they're hiding behind dark glasses.'

'I. Am. Not. Hiding. Behind. Anything,' Jessica said stiffly, thoroughly unnerved, which of course had been his intention as she well knew. 'The glare from the sun makes my eyes water.'

'Rubbish.' He stretched out on the towel next to her, and

out of the corner of her eye she could see a few curious
looks coming their way. Mary and Elizabeth had both
stopped reading their books—what a coincidence—and
were staring across in their direction, attempting to look as
though they were admiring the general scenery.

'You are going to start rumours,' Jessica told him in a
low, furious voice. He had shoved the sunglasses behind
him, firmly out of reach.

'What kind of rumours?'

'Rumours…that…that…' She spluttered into silence,
and he gave her a slow, lazy smile.

'I'm merely sitting down to have a chat with one of my
employees.'

Jessica ground her teeth together in sheer frustration.

'So…what do you think of this little slice of paradise?'
He lay down with his hands behind his head, and her eyes
reluctantly followed the long, athletic lines of his body.

'It's beautiful. You're very lucky to have this as a bolt-
hole. Do you come here often?'

'When I need to unwind.'

'Good. Well.' Making her mind up, she stood up and he
promptly yanked her back down in such a smooth, unhurried gesture that she half toppled onto him, but managed to
straighten herself with the speed of light.

'Not so fast. I'm enjoying our little conversation.'

'Glad one of us is,' Jessica muttered indignantly.

'And so are you. Why pretend? You might want to scurry
away like a terrified rabbit…'

'Me? A terrified rabbit?'

'Oh, yes. Once you're dragged away from your work—'

'I am perfectly controlled, inside and outside the working
environment!' she snapped, cursing the heat that had
flooded through her.

'You mean, you'd dearly like to be. Your face lets you

down, though,' he murmured thoughtfully. 'It's too expressive.'

'That's never been a problem before I met you!' she blurted out truthfully, horrified into sudden silence by the admission. 'You...you...'

'Yes? I'm all ears.'

'Are absolutely insufferable. And I'm going to swim.'

She stood up and headed down towards the water, burning with embarrassment.

She shouldn't have worn the bikini, though she actually looked better with fewer clothes. She had the sort of long, slender body that was rendered shapeless by too many layers. She should, she thought, finally reaching the water's edge with relief, have stuck to the one hideous one-piece she had brought with her, but then how on earth could she have known that he would turn up like a bad penny?

She would simply remain in the water, splashing about in an aimless fashion, until he vacated her towel. Every so often she glanced in his direction, half expecting him to come in for a dip while she was there, but eventually he eased himself off her towel, gave her a brief wave and strolled down the beach, stopping to talk for quite some time to Mary and Elizabeth, then further along to the remainder of the crowd whose high-spirited activities had become progressively more sluggish in the heat.

Jessica watched from the water, alternately floating on her back, then ducking and swimming under the cool, clear sea, then when the coast was clear she emerged with relief.

Why had he decided to come? Was it because he knew that his presence would throw her into a state of turmoil, and he found the condition highly amusing? He had said as much. He saw her as an object of curiosity and that thought stung. It made her feel like a freak and perhaps to him she was.

When she strolled back into the house an hour later it was to find an impromptu buffet laid out on the extensive back lawns, and Bruno holding court.

Ronnie, clad only in her bikini top, which had clearly been designed as a cleavage enhancer, and a colourful sarong skirt, was flirting in a kittenish manner, which involved lots of giggling, and even Carla, who was engaged and rarely strayed from the topic of her fiancé, was laughing at something Bruno was saying, and looking rather coy.

Jessica, having thrown some baggy shorts and an even baggier tee shirt over her bikini, helped herself to a plate of food and positioned herself on the sidelines, politely listening to Bruno's amusing accounts of trips he had taken abroad and still burning from what he had said to her earlier on.

'Sheep's eyes,' he was saying now, to an audience that appeared to be hanging on to his every word, 'I assure you, are most definitely one of life's more acquired tastes.'

He glanced in her direction, his eyes lingering momentarily on her outfit, which left everything to the imagination, and she feigned an interested look in what he had been saying.

'And have you any unpleasant experiences to recount from trips abroad, Jessica?'

Of course, he *would* involve her in the conversation, wouldn't he? Knowing that that would be the very last thing she wanted.

'Well...there was the time I very nearly had my leg chewed off by a school of barracuda while swimming in the Indian Ocean,' she said to no one in particular. 'Fortunately I was rescued in the nick of time by a passing helicopter, which airlifted me to safety. The perfect rescue if it weren't for the fact that we immediately flew into a freak storm and very nearly crashed. As it was the pilot lost control and fainted and I had to take over.'

'No!' Ronnie cried in amazement, and Jessica grinned at her.

'You're right. No. My trips abroad have all been spectacularly uneventful, I'm afraid.' At which point, with lunch out of the way, the party broke up, going in different directions, mostly indoors to recover from the effects of the morning sun.

Jessica retired to a bench under a tree to finish eating, and gave a little sigh of resignation as Bruno approached her and then proceeded to sit down next to her.

'This will start the rumour mill going,' he said with amusement. 'If this house had net curtains, then I'm sure a few of them would be twitching.'

'Ha, ha, I'm glad you find the thought of that funny.' She stabbed a piece of tomato and stuck it in her mouth.

'Did you have a nice swim this morning?' he asked, and she threw him a sidelong glance.

'Very nice, thank you.'

'I must say, I was impressed by your exciting anecdote about avoiding death by barracuda in the Indian Ocean. Well, until you said that you'd fabricated the whole thing.'

'Which you had known from the start anyway,' she said, sticking her empty plate on the bench next to her and wondering whether it was her imagination or whether he was flirting with her. It was hard to tell with a man like Bruno because he was intrinsically charming. He had the ability to invite the illusion that you were somehow special, simply because when he conversed he had the knack of making you feel as though every pore in his body were focused on whatever you might be saying.

You'd be a fool, of course, to be taken in by any such illusion.

'True,' he said lazily, stretching one arm along the back of the bench, and tilting his face up to the sun, which speckled through the leaves of the tree.

'Because,' Jessica said coolly, 'hard-working career girls like me who have no time for anything exciting in their lives couldn't possibly have exciting adventures, could we?'

Once the words were out of her mouth, she couldn't quite believe that she had said them. What had possessed her? She sounded like a teenager suffering a fit of pique, instead of a mature adult who had her life totally under control.

It was just...that he made her feel, somehow, as though she had missed the boat somewhere along the line. As though there was a huge, exciting life out there, happening to other people, while she remained locked indoors, too scared to venture out. She wasn't sure why she felt that way, but she knew that she never had until he had come along. He was just so *damned charismatic*. She had watched all the faces at lunchtime, focused on him, alight with enthusiasm.

'That remark,' he told her, not bothering to look at her when he spoke, 'has absolutely nothing to do with anything I said, and everything to do with how you feel about yourself.'

'That's utter nonsense and you know it,' Jessica muttered uncomfortably. Rather than risk going down this route of personal confrontation, from which, she knew, she would emerge the loser, she decided to change the topic of conversation altogether. She even managed to inject a note of cheeriness in her voice when she asked him about the island and the house.

'Who maintains it when you're not around?' she asked. Aside from the house, there were extensive grounds, and they were well tended. She suspected that, in the tropics, foliage grew at a rate of knots. He would need a full-time gardener just to stop the place from becoming a jungle.

'I employ three gardeners, who work all year round.' He yawned, which made her feel like yawning as well. It was the heat. 'And when I'm not here, Vicky and Sandy, the housekeepers who are here at the moment, come across twice a week by boat to make sure that everything's ticking over nicely with the house. But it's used frequently. Friends, family, et cetera.'

'This heat is sleep-inducing, isn't it?' she said politely, already making her excuses for leaving, and he turned to look at her, reading her mind.

'I always think there's something particularly time-wasting about sleeping during the day, don't you?'

'No.'

'Why don't we go for a little walk? Something I want to show you.'

'What?' Panic.

'Come on.' He stood up and waited for her to follow suit, which she didn't. 'You make remarks,' he said mildly, 'about being thought of as unexciting, but you refuse to stray from your carefully monitored path, don't you?'

'And what is *that* supposed to mean?' She looked up at him, shading her eyes with her hand.

'I tell you that I want to show you something and your immediate reaction isn't one of curiosity, it's one of wariness. You act as though anything you aren't familiar with is necessarily going to be unpleasant. Isn't that why you didn't want to come over here? Too scared to try anything out of the ordinary?' He began walking away, and Jessica sprang to her feet and stumbled behind him, matching her pace to his, arms folded, with a look of tight-lipped defensiveness on her face.

'I don't think that's fair!' she panted, wiping her forehead with the back of her hand. Over her bikini, which she had kept on, the tee shirt was clinging to her body like a second skin.

'No, but it worked.' He raised his eyebrows tellingly. 'That's the problem about the truth. Gets a person running around after it, hell-bent on proving it's a lie.'

'That's a ridiculous, homespun piece of amateur psychology!'

'Well, you *could* always retire for a siesta,' he said mildly.

'I never said I wanted a siesta!'

They were inside the house now, which was thankfully much cooler, and she glanced briefly around to see whether anyone was lurking nearby, but wherever they were it wasn't in the sprawling bowels of the living area.

'Well...' he stuck his hands into the pockets of his khaki-coloured shorts and appeared to give the matter some thought '...you could always retreat to the very furthest corner of the house with a book.'

'You are...impossible!'

'Because I'm doing you the great disservice of making you think? Truth hurts. Isn't that how the saying goes?'

'Because you think you can swan around making sweeping assumptions about other people! Because you think you have a right to air your views, whether someone wants to hear them or not!' She started to turn away, and he reached out and caught her by her arm, spinning her around to face him.

'Tell me something, has *no one* ever criticised you in your life before?'

Jessica stood absolutely still, red-faced and trembling. 'In abundance,' she heard herself say. 'About the way I looked and the friends I never had because I was never allowed them, and the grades I got which were never quite good enough.'

'Your father?' Bruno asked quietly.

'He was never satisfied. With any of us. I...I...' Jessica bit her lip and told herself that if she cried, if she did the unthinkable and burst into tears, she would take a vow of silence and retreat to the nearest convent.

'Which makes sense.' He took a strand of her hair and pushed it away from her face. 'Look, you go relax. I'll see you later, I'm sure.'

He began walking away, and after a moment's hesitation she ran after him and said, without preamble, 'If the offer still stands, I'll come with you to see...whatever it was you wanted to show me...'

'You sure about that?' he asked, looking at her narrowly, and she nodded.

They walked out together, onto the beach, while her mind furiously went over what he had said to her and what she had said to him. He was right, she thought with a pang of shame: she projected a veneer of hard, single-minded ambition and she had fought hard to get where she was. But her detachment was off-putting, and she knew that her demeanour did not invite criticism. Oh, she was fine if something critical was said about her work, but she did not encourage personal criticism. Bruno Carr was the first man who had ever bluntly spoken his mind, and she had, she thought, confused, dropped all her defences and confided in him.

They turned the corner of the beach and continued walking as the lush vegetation became denser.

'Small question,' Jessica said, determined now to be bright and cheerful and to pretend that their conversation had never taken place. 'Should we have a map?'

He turned and raised both eyebrows expressively and she

felt a shiver of awareness dart down her spine. He was perspiring and there was a certain animal heat about him that made her limbs feel slightly uncontrolled.

'Map? Map?' He gave her a wolfish grin. 'Only wimps need maps! I can orient myself anywhere in the world just by glancing at the sun.'

'Good job it's a very small island,' she returned with a shaky laugh. 'That has the ring of famous last words before two people end up hopelessly lost and going round in circles.' She had an insane desire to wipe a trickle of perspiration from him with one finger, and lick it away.

'Oh, ye of little faith.' He turned away, whistling under his breath, and continued weaving his way through the bush and coconut trees until they finally arrived at another strip of white sand, narrower and more coral-strewn than the area by the house. Moored to a tree was a small boat, with a small engine and a couple of oars inside. Jessica stared at it, uncertain as to what her reaction ought to be. It wasn't what she had been expecting. She had thought he had wanted to point out something of peculiar natural beauty—a rare flower, or tree or shrub. Certainly not a boat.

'*Et voilà!*' he said, turning to her, and she looked at him dubiously.

'It's a boat,' she said finally. 'What's it doing tethered way out here?'

'Sheer cussedness on my part.' He began loosening the rope that secured it to the tree trunk. 'I enjoy the sweaty, physical exertion of getting here. Also stops it being used randomly by visitors when they come.'

'What are you doing?' she asked, stifling another of those little panic attacks that seemed to strike whenever she was faced with the prospect of being alone with him.

'What does it look like?' He glanced briefly at her. 'I'm going to take you to a part of the island that's only accessible by boat.' He pushed it towards the water and she watched his sinewy body with trancelike concentration, then she gathered herself and smiled. No overreacting, she told herself. No ridiculous teenage hysterics—he's being the perfect host and wants to show me as much as he can because he knows that when I get back to England I'll return to my nose to the grindstone.

'Great!'

He looked at her with amusement. 'Hop in.'

'The engine works, doesn't it?' She climbed into the boat which was bobbing in the shallow, seaweedy water and he climbed in after her.

'Let's hope so. Rowing can be tiring work.'

'But doubtless something you see as another challenge.' She was looking around as she spoke, and missed the glint of laughter in his eyes.

'Doubtless.' He pulled twice on the cord to start the engine, and it put-putted into life with the high-pitched whine of a sewing machine. Then he sat back down on the bench facing her and picked up speed as they cleared the shallow water and headed out to sea. He explained the layout of the island, and as he spoke she looked off to the horizon and tried to ignore her heart hammering madly against her rib-cage. Within five minutes he slowed the engine and headed inland towards a cove, very small, with a backdrop of thick trees and bush. The water was clear enough for her to see the grains of sand at the bottom of the sea bed. Swimming-pool water. Idyllic. But deserted.

'Great place to swim,' he announced as he killed the engine and allowed the boat to drift towards shore. 'The water's incredibly warm just here.'

'Brilliant!' Jessica said faintly.

'Isn't it?' He stood up, steadying himself, then stepped out of the boat and pulled it up onto the sand. There was that thread of laughter in his voice that made her think that he could read her mind, see inside her head to every thought. 'I knew you'd agree!'

Tentatively she climbed out, keeping her eyes firmly averted from him.

'And don't look so terrified,' he whispered in her ear, making her jump, 'the sea is clear of man-eating barracuda. Relax. Nothing around here bites...' He gave a low laugh, then moved away from her. 'It's absolutely perfect.'

Yes, she thought. Wasn't it?

# CHAPTER SIX

BRUNO stripped off his shirt, then his shorts, and Jessica was relieved to see that he was wearing a pair of swimming trunks underneath. Dark green, and low slung, so that she could see the arrow of dark hair running from his navel downwards, disappearing beneath the trunks.

How on earth was he so *bronzed*? She wondered whether he had Italian or Spanish blood in him. He certainly bore no passing resemblance to any English man she had ever seen on a beach. She had long come to the conclusion that English men on beaches were not sights for sore eyes. With no clothes to hide them, their whiteness was almost blinding. Even men who looked passable enough in their suits were rendered laughable when caught with nothing on but a pair of trunks on a beach somewhere.

She retreated to the shade of a coconut tree and looked at Bruno out of the corner of her eye. He had strolled towards the water's edge, and was obviously contemplating swimming out.

'Why are you lurking there?' he shouted over to her, and Jessica hurriedly plastered her gaze somewhere else, shading her eyes with her hands. 'You must be baking with all those clothes on!' She saw the flash of white teeth and felt the familiar bristle as she caught the laughter in his voice.

'I'm fine,' she told him. She could feel the sweat trickling under her armpits and at the back of her neck, where some coils of hair were glued to her skin.

'Join me for a swim!' he commanded, walking towards her, and she eyed him warily. There was no one around, and it was very unlikely that anyone would suddenly appear on the scene. For a small island, this was a remarkably remote spot.

'Can't.' She flashed him a smile. He moved, she thought, with the grace of a panther.

'Why not?' He raked his fingers through his hair and half turned away, so that he was looking out to sea, his face in profile.

'Sun's too hot out there. This is the worst time to be in the sun if you're fair, and I forgot to bring my sun cream.' She shrugged her shoulders helplessly. 'So you go ahead and have a swim. I must say, the water looks very inviting.' She sighed wistfully and gazed at the calm, turquoise sea, as clear as a pool. 'Maybe I'll have a dip in a minute.'

'Well, you're probably right,' Bruno told her sympathetically. 'You just stay well wrapped up, and take refuge in some shade.' He folded his arms and flicked his eyes over her. 'You know, I have a tin with some oil clothes on the boat...I could always rig up a hat of sorts for further protection...' So much for that air of sympathy, she thought crossly.

'That won't be necessary.' She headed off for the nearest tree, sat down, and watched as he walked at a leisurely pace towards the sea, then pushed out, moving quickly away from shore, until his form became smaller and smaller.

She felt a sharp pull of anxiety when he disappeared altogether.

Where the hell was he?

She could remember him telling them that there were no currents around the beach because of coral reefs further out, but then, since when was he an expert on the tidal movements of the ocean?

She stood up, squinting against the glare, her body reaching forward as she tried to distinguish any bobbing figure that might be his. When he finally surfaced, waving at her, she clicked her tongue with irritation and promptly sat back down. Then she lay on her back, stretched her legs out in front of her, and closed her eyes.

Her heart was still beating fast at the thought that he might have been swept out to sea, even though she knew that it had been a ridiculous, passing urge to be worried about him.

If there was one person in the world who could take care of himself, it was Bruno Carr. An ocean current would have to be particularly reckless to think that it could carry him away. She doubted that he had ever been carried away by anything or anyone in his life. His life was utterly and completely in control. Events were things, she imagined, which he manipulated for his own ends, just as he no doubt manipulated the people around him.

A slight breeze blew, and without opening her eyes she hoisted her tee shirt over her head, then folded it roughly and shoved it behind her, pillow-style.

She was on the verge of drifting off into a delicious doze when she felt a spattering of water on her, and her eyes flew open.

There he was, standing over her, and with the sun behind him his face was thrown into shadow. She jerked up into a sitting position, ready to throw him the well-rehearsed smile, to find that he wasn't smiling at her. That ironic, amused grin which seemed permanently to play on his lips whenever he was in her company had been replaced by something else.

He was looking at her. *Really looking at her.* She could feel her skin begin to prickle, and she had to clear her throat before she spoke because she knew that, if she didn't, her words would trip over one another in nervousness.

What was he playing at?

'Good swim?' she asked, in a high voice, and he didn't say anything. 'Wish I could have ventured in...' she volunteered in a cheery voice.

'You look very different when you're asleep.'

'What?' Jessica looked at him, shocked by the intimacy of the remark.

'You heard me.' He sat down alongside her, and every nerve in her body went into immediate overdrive. He leaned against the trunk of the coconut tree, with his long legs stretched out in front of him, loosely crossed at the ankles, and proceeded to look at her.

'How long were you...standing there...staring at me?' She tried to inject some righteous anger in her voice, but failed. She was very much aware that if she shifted a few inches to her left, she would touch him. The thought of that sent a wave of faintness through her.

'Not staring...observing.'

'Oh, right. And the difference is enormous.'

She couldn't maintain his stare, so she turned away and looked out across the white sand, across the water to the sharp blue line of the horizon.

She couldn't believe that she was sitting here, her toes sifting through the castor-sugar sand, next to a man who had swept into her life like a tornado, and feeling things that she knew were absolutely out of order. It was almost as though the change in the scenery had cast a spell on her, released some invisible plug on her emotions.

*Why, for God's sake, was her heart doing such feeble things? Beating like a damn drum just because a man had looked at her?*

'When you're asleep—'

'I wasn't *asleep*. I had my eyes closed.'

'When you're asleep,' he drawled, paying no notice to her interruption, 'you look soft and defenceless.'

'Everyone looks defenceless when they're asleep,' Jessica said shortly, uncomfortable with the conversation. Her fingers played restlessly with the edge of her shorts.

'What made you stop trusting the human race?' he asked softly, and without warning he placed one finger under her chin and tilted her face towards his.

Jessica opened her mouth to say something clever, but when she tried to speak she found that her vocal cords had dried up. She thought she could hear her heart, if that was possible. She could almost hear the surge of her blood crashing through her veins.

'Was it just your father or was there a man as well to compound the problem?' he asked.

'No.' She made a small movement to look away, but he stilled her.

'What, then?'

'I...' She couldn't believe that she was having this conversation. Worse. That she felt compelled to confide in him. The heat was magical, turning her brains to mush. 'I'm afraid my childhood...left a lot to be desired.'

'Your father...'

'Was a tyrant.' There was fierceness in her voice, and she frowned at him. 'He ruled the household with a rod of iron. We weren't allowed...to do anything. Running in the house, shouting...' Her memories were so real that she felt as though she had been swept back into time. 'We all crept around like mice, too afraid to even laugh when he was around.' She looked nervously at him, waiting for him to say something dismissive about what she had told him, but his gaze was steady and unfaltering, and utterly serious.

'The worst of it was...my mum...she must have been full of laughter once...but by the time I grew up, all that had been sucked out of her. All the joy…gone.' She met his eyes without flinching. 'He fooled around, you see. Mum was someone who stayed at home, raising the children and looking after the house, and all the other women…' She shook her head, bewildered now, as she had been then, when she had first overheard her parents arguing behind a semi-closed door. 'He saw nothing wrong in what he did, and when Mum eventually tried to leave, she found that she couldn't. Her self-confidence had taken such a battering over the years that she no longer had any faith in herself. So, you see…' she shrugged lightly and blinked '…I learned pretty fast that it was up to me to sort my life out. I couldn't trust anyone else to do it for me. Aren't I a sad creature?' She attempted a laugh, but it was wobbly and unconvincing.

He stroked some hair from her face, and his fingers burnt her flesh.

'Absolutely not.' He gave her a slow smile. 'No more than the rest of us sad creatures that inhabit this good planet of ours.'

'Are you telling me that you had a miserable childhood?'

'Virtually trouble free,' he admitted, and she gave a low, shaky laugh.

'Now, why do you think I would have guessed as much?' she asked lightly.

'No idea. You tell me.'

She hoped he wasn't seriously expecting an answer to that.

'Shouldn't we think about leaving?'

'Why?'

'Why? Because…'

'Ah, those rumours…might start flying around again…'

'No!'

'Well, then...' he shook his head thoughtfully '...I guess the sun is beginning to make you feel a bit dizzy...'

'The sun's fine...' Enough of a cool breeze to dilute the intensity.

He smiled, a slow, lazy smile, and raised one eyebrow expressively. 'Then the only other reason I can think of is that you're afraid to stay here alone with me...are you? I make you nervous, don't I? I can see it in your body movements. The minute I get too close, you shift a bit just in case I touch you. Why do you think that is? Are you scared that I might make a pass at you...?'

Jessica could feel herself holding her breath. She could also feel the slow, burning flush that spread outwards and upwards, engulfing her.

'I'm afraid of no such thing!' she protested, instantly mortified at the thought that he might be laughing at her, feeling sorry for her with her silly sob stories.

'You should be...'

It took a few seconds for the impact of what he had said to sink in, but when it had her mouth flew open and remained parted. A slow, hot excitement uncurled inside her, like a spiral of smoke. The first sign of a conflagration.

He cupped her face with his hand, and then everything seemed to happen in slow motion. His head lowering to hers, his mouth touching hers, then the feel of his tongue as the kiss became deeper and more urgent.

She had never felt this response before, had never felt dizzy with want.

She reached up and clasped her hands behind his head, and returned his kiss with an abandoned passion she never would have thought possible.

Their tongues met and clashed, wet and thrusting, and she moaned as his fingers slid under the strap of her bikini top, tugging it down.

'God knows, I've wanted to do this…' he groaned, his voice husky and thick. She arched back, fiddling with the clasp at the back, until the bikini top was off and her breasts, larger than they appeared under the camouflage of clothes, hung unrestrained.

Her nipples had hardened into aching peaks, and she shuddered uncontrollably when his fingers began rubbing and teasing.

'Big nipples,' he murmured into her ear. 'I like that.' His tongue flicked wetly in her ear, sending electric currents through her, and then he began licking her neck, while he massaged one full breast with his hand.

In the olden days, ladies swooned. Jessica thought that this must have been what it felt like. As though all her bones had turned to liquid.

She cradled his head, squirming and gasping as he trailed his mouth lower, along her collar-bone. The anticipation of that mouth suckling on a nipple was akin to ecstasy. She urged his head down, and groaned softly as wetness enfolded the pink, throbbing peak. He sucked, pulling her breast into his mouth, arousing the nipple with his tongue, and she ran her hands over his hard, muscled torso, loving the feel of his skin beneath her palms.

'Feel good?' he asked, and she opened her eyes and smiled drowsily at him.

It felt so good that she couldn't bear his mouth away from her body, and, sensing her need, he slowly continued to explore her breasts, running his tongue on the underside, nibbling their softness, teasing her nipples until she wanted to scream.

He slid his hand underneath the elasticised waistband of her shorts, and pulled them down. She wriggled, then kicked them off, parting her legs.

Her wetness down there surprised her. How was it that

she had never reached these amazing heights of pleasure before? Was it because, for the first time in her life, she felt as though she had truly relinquished all control?

He placed the flat of his hand between her thighs and gently rubbed. In response, she reached down and found his pulsating manhood, looking at him so that she could enjoy his own surrender of self-control.

'Take your time,' he murmured, his eyes burning, and she sighed.

Time, she knew, was something they had very little of. Before they knew it, it would have crept up on them, and they would have to leave this idyll behind. But for the moment she put all such thoughts to the back of her head as she eased her body down, down so that she could explore him the way he had been exploring her.

Her mouth drifted sensually over the flat planes of his stomach, feeling his muscles tense and harden under her, then she nuzzled his erect member, licking the shaft, then covering it with her mouth, and as she did so she felt him stiffen, and his breathing become more rapid.

With her hands, she stroked and caressed him, wanting to give him as much pleasure as he had given her, wanting to take her time as well so that what was happening between them, remarkable as it was, would stretch out as long as possible.

She realised that she didn't want this to end. She didn't want to roll away from him and face the present once again.

Sex, which had always been something pleasant enough that had tended to happen at the end of an evening out, had been transformed into something wild and hungry and surging with passion and yearning.

She could feel her body reaching out for him and when he moved to urge her onto her back, she eased her bikini bottom off, so that her soft, blonde, damp curls were exposed to the balmy air.

This ultimate intimacy was a first for her. She watched his dark head descend lower, until his mouth nuzzled against those damp curls.

His tongue found her swollen, throbbing bud and flicked against it, and she moaned and moved against him, pushing herself up. One hand was entwined in his hair, the other loosely thrown over her face, as she panted under the waves of exquisite pleasure rushing through her.

She gyrated her hips, and the pressure of his tongue became stronger. His hands were spread underneath her firm buttocks, and he urged her on until the waves of pleasure became an irresistible crashing force.

She felt her body tense and tighten, then shudder uncontrollably.

But still he kept licking, teasing every ounce of energy out of her body, so that the one powerful climax merged into a series of utterly wonderful shivers of intense fulfilment.

When he finally thrust into her, a deep excitement filled her, unlike anything she had ever experienced before. His mouth covered hers in a hungry, urgent kiss, while one hand cupped her breast and massaged it.

Jessica cried out, a deep, hoarse cry that didn't sound as though it could possibly come from her, and as she felt him reach his own soaring heights her body stiffened in wild response.

How long had time stood still?

When she next opened her eyes, it was to find him looking down at her with the same drowsy contentment that she was feeling and she gave him a tremulous smile.

'Perhaps I will risk a swim in this heat after all,' she murmured, tracing his features with one finger, which he grasped and put into his mouth, so that the smile became a giggle of delight.

'Sounds like a good idea.' He eased himself off her, and they faced one another on their sides.

'If I can only find the energy to get up.'

'Feeling a little drained, are you?'

'Just a bit.' She ran her hand lightly along his side, and then along his upper thigh. She felt, amazingly, as though she had been asleep all her adult life, and was now awake for the first time. Her body was still tingling in the aftermath of their lovemaking.

'Well, no time like the present,' he said, without moving, and he lay flat on his back with his hands folded behind his head and stared upwards for a few seconds, before transferring his gaze to her.

She moved to start slipping back on the bikini, and he stopped her.

'But what if someone comes along?' she whispered nervously as they stood up and began strolling down to the water. She glanced back over her shoulder, and he laughed and rumpled her hair, which looked a mess.

'I guess they'd be in for a shock.'

'That's fine for you to say,' Jessica told him sternly, kicking at the water as they stepped in. 'When we get back to England...' it seemed a million miles away, and the thought of it filled her with a sudden, shocking feeling of disappointment, which she immediately stifled '...you'll vanish back into that ivory tower of yours, but I'll be left with the whispering and knowing looks...'

'True,' he agreed readily. 'But what's a little whispering and a few knowing looks to a determined young woman like yourself?' He grinned and began splashing her with water, and she returned the favour with equal enthusiasm until they were both drenched, and all thoughts of being overseen were lost in the sheer physical activity of swimming.

Swimming and touching, soft, wet strokes that made her want to return to the little patch of sand under the tree and make love to him all over again.

Her hair hung down to her waist like a sheath of dark gold, and the sun was so hot that after only a few minutes with her head above water she could feel it beginning to dry off.

As they emerged from the water he held her from behind, his arms enfolding her, and she gasped as his fingers slipped down between her thighs, caressing her.

'Anyone could be spying on us!' she protested, not struggling very hard to resist because his fingers were rapidly firing her body into a wet, willing response.

'Don't be so worried,' he murmured, sweeping her hair to one side and bending to kiss her neck. 'This little spot is surprisingly difficult to find if you don't know precisely where to go. Trust me.'

'Trust you? Isn't that something of a tall order?' She twisted around to give him a sceptical, amused look from under her lashes, and he grinned back obligingly.

'I sense criticism in that remark.' They held hands and began walking back towards their clothes, which lay strewn at the scene of their lovemaking.

It hadn't been meant as criticism, or even to be taken seriously, but now that he had offered that observation she suddenly gave some consideration to what had just happened between them. For a minute, she had taken flight, but the earth was still under her feet and sooner or later she would have to land.

She thoughtfully slipped back on her sandy bikini and her even sandier shorts and then sat down, hugging her knees and waiting while he dressed and sat back down next to her.

'Actually,' she said slowly, turning to face him, 'I wasn't being critical.'

'But...? That expression on your face is telling me that there's a postscript attached to that little statement of yours...'

'This feels so unreal,' she started, with hesitation. She dropped one hand to the sand and began sifting through it, watching it filter through her fingers like castor sugar. 'Look...I feel you should know that I...' She sighed and mentally made an effort to work out where she was going with this one. 'I'm not the kind of girl who makes a habit of this sort of thing...' She gave an unsteady laugh and felt a rush of confusion at what she had just said. Not only was she *not* the sort of girl who did *this sort of thing*, she was not the sort of girl who had ever even contemplated it.

So how had it all happened so easily?

'I know.'

'Because your experience is with girls who would *easily* do that sort of thing?' She couldn't help it but she felt a stab of jealousy so deep that it was a physical pain in her chest.

'What do you want me to say to that?'

'The truth?' This conversation was not going where she had expected it to. Ten minutes previously, they had been swimming naked in the crystal waters, and she had felt as though she had no cares in the world. Now reality had come barging through and was refusing to budge until it had been dealt with.

Why did that fill her with such a sense of anger and regret? She had never had a problem facing up to reality, but now she wished that it would just go away and leave her alone.

'Okay, the truth is that I haven't had a string of women who particularly balk at the prospect of going to bed with a man. If you want to call them easy, then you can. So, as far as my trustworthiness goes, I guess it's never had to be put to the test.' He expelled a long breath and looked at her with utter seriousness. 'I work damn hard and I've never sought out the responsibility of a committed relationship. I never felt the need for it.'

'Well, at least you don't have a problem with honesty.' A breeze wafted and blew her hair into chaotic semi-dry tendrils around her face.

He hadn't told her anything that she hadn't already figured out for herself, but she still felt a little shocked at the brutality of his frankness.

'I try not to. Lying just ends up in a knotty situation.'

'So this weekend…'

'Can be whatever you want it to be.'

Jessica stared out to sea, curling a strand of hair around her finger. She knew what was on offer. A temporary liaison on an island that inspired magic.

She desperately wanted to ask him what happened once the weekend drew to a close, but she already knew the answer to that one. He neither wanted nor needed anything permanent in his life. In fact, she doubted he even wanted anything that remotely smelled of permanence. She wasn't his type, nor was he hers, but for a few days they could let the spell that had been cast run its course.

'What do *you* want?' she asked curiously, turning to look at him.

'You.'

'A holiday fling,' she said pensively. The way he looked at her filled her with a heady, drowning sensation. She looked away and distractedly flicked some sand with one finger, watching as it sprayed into the air.

'A time to remember.'

'Oh, very poetic.' Jessica laughed, not caring to look into the future beyond the weekend. He ran his fingers along her spine and she shivered. 'Perhaps we should be getting back.'

'I take it that's your answer?'

'I don't know *what* my answer is.'

And she truly didn't. But for the remainder of the day she felt his presence with such force that it left her breathless. This really was the stuff of memories. She didn't think that she would ever forget the way he made her feel, the way he sent her senses spinning into orbit.

She could feel his eyes on her, even when he was talking to everyone else, and it was like being touched. As dusk turned into inky blackness, and food was eaten and alcohol consumed, and the noise levels rose, the undercurrent running between them was like the silent buzz of electricity. Her eyes were drawn compulsively to him, as though her body had tuned into its own peculiar radio signal, but she only realised what she wanted to do when, as the last of the straggling crew drifted off to their bedroom, the worse for wear, she lingered behind, waiting and watching.

And even then, there were still the remnants of hesitation.

Was she cut out for this kind of thing? Was she fashioned for the one-off fling, no strings attached? She must surely be, she reasoned fiercely to herself, because she certainly wasn't fashioned for the whole marriage bit.

She didn't want commitment any more than he did, so why was she so scared at the prospect of this brief, intense fling, followed by nothing?

'Not heading off to bed?' She heard his voice from behind her, and jumped. He was switching off lights, checking the doors to make sure that everywhere was closed. In the darkness, he was a tall, shadowy figure, lounging indolently against the wall, his hands stuck in his pockets.

As she looked at him she could feel her breath quickening, and she raised her hand to her throat, forcing herself to be calm.

'Are you?' she asked in a ridiculously high voice.

'Actually…' he pushed himself away from the wall and walked slowly towards her, and with every step closer she could feel her heart rate accelerate '…I was thinking about a stroll on the beach. Care to join me?'

They both knew what he was asking, and after only a few seconds' hesitation she nodded.

'I've never strolled on a beach at midnight,' she confessed. He was now standing so close to her that she could feel her nipples hardening, pushing against her shirt, aroused simply at the thought of what he could do to her.

'It's quite an experience,' he murmured, and his voice was like a caress—a soft, velvety caress.

They silently left the house and walked down to the beach, then down to the water's edge so that the sea lapped against their bare feet. Everything around them was dark. The sea, the sky, the silhouettes of the trees like swaying black figures. They began walking away from the house, until they had left it behind. With every step, she could feel that thread of pulsating excitement growing stronger and stronger.

When he finally turned to her and cupped her face in his hands, she breathed a sigh of satisfaction, tilting her head upwards, parting her lips to meet his mouth as it descended and moved against hers in a soft, lingering, never-ending kiss.

Tomorrow was a point in time which no longer existed. For the first time in her life the only thing that mattered was the here and now, with no plans for the future, no looking ahead.

She wasn't wearing a bra, and a part of her wondered now whether she hadn't already made her mind up when she had changed clothes earlier in the evening.

His hands slid to her waist, circling it, his thumbs meeting and rubbing her navel, then climbing higher, under the baggy shirt, pushing it up until her breasts were exposed.

They sank slowly, entwined, onto their bed of sand, white and flawless in the burning daylight sun, dark with shadows now.

He buried his head between her breasts, then licked them gently, leaving no part of the full, swelling mounds untouched.

Somehow, this time, the embrace of darkness made things seem less frantic, less urgent. Their actions were unhurried, a slow, thorough exploration of each other's bodies.

He sucked on her nipples, taking his time, savouring their sweetness, and she, in turn, ran her tongue along the firm, hard lines of his torso, marvelling at the ridges of muscles she could feel under her fingers.

The build-up was exquisitely unhurried. It seemed as though everything could last for ever.

When he finally nuzzled the sensitised region between her thighs, she had to stop herself from crying out loud in ecstasy. Even then, there was no rush, no fast rhythm to propel her on to a shuddering, urgent climax. He licked and sucked, and she softly moaned as his tongue found the throbbing bud of her femininity and played with it, gently.

The minutes seemed to stretch on into eternity, with the lapping of the water blending with the lapping of his tongue in her moistness.

There was something shockingly tender about their love-making.

Even as he entered her, his movements were long and deep, and she felt as though her body had been created just for this: to receive him.

She arched back, and he bent forward so that with every thrust his tongue briefly found an engorged nipple and flicked erotically against it. There was no part of her body that wasn't on fire. If two bodies could fuse, then surely theirs must. They were slippery with heat, and she could feel him burning against her. Finally, when she could hold out no longer, his rhythm altered, speeding up, faster and faster until he tensed with the final pleasure just as she felt her body stiffen in response, and she gave a hoarse cry of fulfilment, rolling over so that she could continue the momentum, shuddering uncontrollably as ripple after ripple of pleasure ran through her.

Later, much later, when she rolled to her side and said to him, 'You're right. One weekend, but a weekend that will become the stuff of memories,' she almost felt as though she meant it. Here, in the middle of nowhere, nothing outside seemed to exist, and all her everyday problems appeared petty and meaningless. She could cope with all that, in time.

'And what if I want to see you when we get back?' he asked in a husky voice, and her body stilled.

No, she thought sadly. If only, but what they had here was unique and should remain what it was: a moment in time. She instinctively knew that to prolong their relationship, if that was what it could be called, would be a mistake.

'It wouldn't work,' she whispered softly, blowing into his ear and feeling him stir into life against her. 'You really don't want someone like me, and I'd rather...'

'Quit while you're ahead?'

'Enjoy what we have for what it is,' she amended. A wave of emotion rushed through her, making her feel giddy and faint, and she blinked it away.

'No commitment,' she said quietly. 'It's something neither of us needs.' Or did she? *Did she?* No. It had never been part of her master plan. A weekend she could control, but nothing beyond that.

## CHAPTER SEVEN

'YOU'VE been summoned.' Millie's face wore the same anxious, concerned look that it had held for the interminably fraught last couple of months, but at least, Jessica thought, she had stopped asking her repeatedly if everything was all right.

Everything was not all right. It never would be, and she knew that that was reflected in her every expression, in every move she made, but there seemed to be very little she could do to control that.

'I'm too busy, Mills,' Jessica said, sitting down suddenly and giving in to the overwhelming exhaustion that had been sapping her energy ever since she had returned from that fateful weekend abroad. She rested her head in her open palms and shut her eyes.

'I wish you'd tell me what's wrong,' Millie said worriedly, and Jessica sighed heavily by way of response.

'I'll be fine.'

Not long left to go at the company, then her problems would begin in earnest. She didn't know if she had the strength to face them, but there was no way out.

'Shall I tell Mr Carr that you won't be able to see him?' Millie asked gently, and Jessica's head shot up.

'Bruno Carr wants to see me?' Her voice was hoarse and shocked, and her secretary's face became pinched with consternation. 'Why?' she demanded. 'Why? Why would he want to see me all of a sudden? I've had no contact with the man for weeks and weeks and weeks! What did he say?'

'I don't know,' Millie stammered. 'I'm sorry, Jess...

perhaps he just wants to tell you goodbye personally...'

'How does he know that I'm leaving?' Every aching muscle in her body had sprung into life, filling her with a dreadful sense of apprehension.

How could he still do this to her?

When they had parted company all that time ago, she had cheerfully believed every word she had said to him. She had convinced herself that their very brief fling had been everything and nothing, and all that she had needed. Just what the doctor had ordered, she had told herself, every time his image crept into her head and wreaked havoc with her thoughts.

She barely knew the man, she had thought, and the fact that he seemed to have stuck in her brain was absolutely nothing to worry about. She was not accustomed to having a weekend lover. Of course, she would find it a little difficult to get out of her mind. She wasn't made of stone, after all.

It wasn't even that they were soul mates, she lectured repeatedly to herself, when the hours became days, and the days turned into weeks, and the thought of him still managed to evoke feelings of loss and misery. Time would cure her of her stupidity.

But time, she had discovered, had joined hands with fate and both were conspiring to turn her life on its head.

'He owns this company, Jess...' Millie's voice was confused and agitated, and Jessica knew just what she was thinking: The boss has finally lost it. She's been a mess for the past few weeks, and now she's finally waved goodbye to her sanity.

Jessica cleared her throat, looked up, and made an attempt to speak with at least a semblance of self-control.

'You're right. I'll see him right away.' She watched as

her secretary's expression of worry changed into one of relief. Of course, she had no intention of going to see Bruno Carr, but Millie wasn't to know that.

She stood up, smoothed her hair neatly behind her ears, and plastered a cheerful smile on her face.

'Where is he?' Polite look, a little quizzical, but definitely composed. Millie, she thought, must think I'm deranged.

'At his office. He said that he expects you within the hour.'

Fat chance.

'I'll go immediately.' She glanced at her desk, with the papers covering most of the available free space, and randomly selected a couple which she handed to her secretary. A couple of months ago, she would have been invigorated at the prospect of the work lying in front of her. Now, she couldn't care less. She had an insane urge to sweep her hand across the smooth, hard, wooden surface and watch all those little bits of paper swirl helplessly into the waste-paper basket on the ground. 'Reply to these for me, would you, Mills? And you'd better cancel my appointment to see James Parker this afternoon. I'm not sure what time I'll be back from seeing Mr Carr. If I get back at all.'

'Of course.'

There, there, there, Jessica wanted to say. Don't you feel better now, Mills? Now that I'm acting in character, even if it's all a charade?

She fetched her jacket from the back of her chair and stuck it on. The weather had finally broken after an endless winter and a spring that had seemed reluctant to part company with the cold. Now it had shed its indecision and was everywhere. New, little buds bursting out in the sunshine, daffodils sticking yellow heads through the grass, coats returned to wardrobes for their annual hibernation. Jessica barely noticed any of it. The sky could have been bright red for all she knew, and the sun could have been purple. She came to work in a daze, worked in a daze and returned home in a daze.

'I'll see you in the morning!' Millie called, and Jessica turned around to look at her.

'Oh, yes. See you in the morning.' Then she was gone. Out of the door and the office and walking briskly towards the underground. Several stops, then finally her own. She thought about Bruno, waiting in his office to see her, and shuddered with relief as her house drew closer.

She had yearned to see him. It was unbelievable how much she had yearned to see him. It was as though their one weekend together had opened her up to emotions she had spent a lifetime suppressing.

Now, she could envisage nothing worse.

She slipped her key into the lock, shut the door behind her, and did what she did every evening recently when she returned from work: kicked her shoes off and then collapsed onto the sofa and closed her eyes. There was a lot to do, but the mere thought of doing any of it made her feel faint. The ironing basket seemed to have taken on a life of its own, and was growing daily. If she didn't do something about it, she knew that she would be forced to contact an ironing service to come and take it all away. There were dishes in the sink, and a few of them had been sitting there for the past two days. She hadn't even bothered to soak them in water, and the grime would have hardened so that when she finally did get around to washing them they would stubbornly refuse to release their greasy layers.

None of it seemed to matter. In her head, the problems churned around and around, mutating and changing and shifting positions, but never going away.

How could they?

From her prone position on the sofa, she gave a little groan and rolled over onto her side, feeling utterly horrible in her work clothes. Her hair was coming undone, and she irritably released it from its tightly coiled bun, running her fingers through it and then draping it over one shoulder.

She could feel herself sliding into sleep when the doorbell sounded. It penetrated her fuggy brain like the sudden buzz of a wasp, and as she blinked her way to the surface became shrill and insistent until she could ignore it no longer.

Shoeless, hair everywhere, she stormed to the front door, yanked it open, and then felt her mouth turn to ash.

'I gave it half an hour,' Bruno said coldly, 'and then I phoned your secretary, to be told that you had left some time ago. To come and see me. At my office. As instructed.' He folded his arms and lounged against the doorframe.

'What have you come here for?' She could control her words, but not the tenor of her voice, and she heard the faint tremble in it with a mixture of disgust and panic.

He was everything and more than she remembered. Taller, leaner, more bronzed, and infinitely more disturbing. She felt suffocated by his presence, literally choking from the impact of seeing him here, on her doorstep. How on earth had she ever been able to tell him goodbye, to inform him that she was not open to his offer of casual mistress once they returned to England, to let him know that he had been no more than a wonderful but temporary liaison? How had she ever thought that she could return to her normal life and put him down to experience?

'To see you,' he informed her, his voice ice. 'I came here because it was obvious that you had left the office with no intention whatsoever of taking a taxi to the City.'

He reached inside his trouser pocket and pulled out a sheet of paper. 'Mind telling me what this is all about?'

It was her letter of resignation. She recognised the paper, and the glimpse of signature at the bottom of the typed page. In the absence of her direct boss, she had made sure to send it to the personnel department, never imagining that it would find its way to Bruno Carr. She should have known better. Hadn't he always made a point of saying how au fait he was with everything that happened in his various companies? Clearly it had been no idle boast.

'Come in.' She stepped aside to let him enter. It was strange seeing him like this after all this time. A wall had developed between them and it hurt to remember how easy they had been with one another. It seemed like a lifetime away. As he brushed past her she could feel her skin crawl, and her pulses began to race.

She didn't know what the hell she was going to tell him, but she knew that he wouldn't leave until she provided him with an answer. Any answer. Any answer but the truth.

'Would you like a cup of tea?' she asked politely. 'Some coffee?' With a change of clothes she could be a waitress, she thought, so impersonal was her voice, and by way of response he threw her a dark, brooding scowl, before walking towards the sitting room and making himself comfortable on one of the chairs.

'I'll pass on the drink,' he told her sarcastically. 'Sorry. I guess that means a little less time for you to try and fabricate an excuse.'

'I wasn't going to do any such thing.' She picked the end of the sofa furthest away from him and sat down. Even at this distance, she could feel him as strongly as if he were touching her.

'How did you get hold of my resignation?' she asked eventually. It was hard to maintain her composure and she found herself leaning forward, her elbows resting on her knees.

Oh, God. She had never envisaged laying eyes on him again. This was her worst nightmare.

'I keep tabs on everything that goes on in my company,' he informed her icily. 'It's my business.'

'Of course.'

'Correct me if I'm wrong,' he said, sitting back and tossing her letter of resignation dismissively on the table between them, 'but the last time I saw you, you were perfectly happy with your job.'

'Things change.' She shrugged and threw him an apologetic smile, which did nothing to alter his thunderous expression. The steady, polite smile on her face slipped a little. 'I decided that the job just wasn't challenging enough for me,' she told him, thinking on her feet, and steering far away from any possible excuse which might encourage him to smell a rat. 'I suppose it was the anticlimax of your court case. I realised that I no longer had anything to get my teeth into.' She could feel herself building up some very convenient momentum with this line of reasoning. It was beginning to sound more and more plausible.

She still couldn't quite meet his eyes though. So, instead, she addressed the space slightly to the left of his ear. Craven but necessary if her heart wasn't to start doing unmanageable things behind her ribcage. She could already feel most of her confident assertions, which she had made repeatedly to herself over the past few weeks—that he was insignificant in her life, a ship that had passed in the night—ebbing away at a furious rate.

'What a period of revelations for you,' he commented acidly.

'Yes. Yes, it was! And what's the problem here anyway?' she snapped, going onto the attack. 'I assume your employees aren't chained to your companies for life! I assume they're at liberty to move on! Tell me, do you subject each and every employee who has the temerity to try and resign to this kind of third degree?' Her heart was pounding and her face was bright red. She could feel it burning as though her whole body were on fire.

She desperately wanted to be angry with him. If need be, she would generate her own spurious argument, because the anger was her only point of protection. She knew that any other reaction would allow memories to seep through, and she couldn't allow that to happen.

'So you were suddenly disillusioned with your job. And I take it that you've already found something else? Or were you so disillusioned that you decided to throw it all in and to heck with the possibility of earning nothing? No,' he said slowly to himself, while she listened to his line of reasoning with helpless frustration. 'Surely not. You've always made such a point of being in control of your life, of needing to be in control of your life, that you'd hardly pack in a hefty pay cheque on wild impulse. Which leaves us with your new job. What is it? I'm all ears.'

He sat back and allowed himself the satisfied smile of the cat that had successfully cornered the mouse.

'I haven't found anything yet,' Jessica muttered under her breath.

'Dear, oh, dear. Now, that makes no sense at all. Does it?'

She said nothing, feeling trapped.

'Which is probably why I don't buy the *I'm suddenly disillusioned* excuse.' He stared at her coolly and with a degree of calculation that made her nervous system go into overdrive. Her mind raced ahead, attempting to pre-empt all possible arguments he could throw at her, but nothing in her head appeared to be working efficiently.

'I really don't care what you buy or don't buy.' Brave words, she thought miserably, if it weren't for the fact they were sabotaged by the shakiness of her voice.

'Sure about that?'

'What are you talking about?'

He folded his arms and surveyed her unhurriedly and dispassionately.

'I find it a bit coincidental that we shared a weekend together, and then suddenly you decide to quit.'

A chill was beginning to crawl up her spine.

'I've always enjoyed crosswords,' he mused pensively. 'I like the challenge posed to the intellect. The knowledge that, however convoluted the clue is, there's an answer and the answer is clear provided your brain's working in the right direction.'

That chill was now spreading outwards, numbing her. She felt as though she were being pulled along behind something very fast and quite unstoppable. She could barely breathe, never mind open her mouth and try to change the course of this remorseless reasoning.

'I looked at your letter of resignation and none of it made any sense,' he continued, relentless and implacable. 'Believe it or not, I did consider your original line of argument, that you had become turned off the nature of the work, but I dismissed that almost immediately for the reasons I gave you.' He smiled, but there was nothing remotely warm about it. Her hands, resting on her knees, felt clammy.

'Which made me wonder whether you had had a falling out with someone you work with, but I was certain that that wasn't the case... Of course, there was the slight chance that you found yourself unable to manage Robert's job, but that wasn't it, was it? I've been keeping tabs on you and I would have been the first to have heard. Which in turn led me to think that perhaps our weekend together meant more to you than you had said at the time.'

She felt her body still. Her brain had turned over that horrifying thought so often in the past few weeks that it had physically hurt, and still the answer to the question eluded her.

'Maybe you'd nurtured cosy little thoughts of togetherness... Maybe that was why you wouldn't contemplate seeing me on a casual basis once we got back...maybe you wanted more than that...much more...' He let the insinuation hang in the air between them, until mortification at the prolonged silence forced her into speech.

'Hardly. But of course you'd find that hard to believe because your ego wouldn't allow it.' She could feel herself on the brink of anger once again, but somehow she couldn't quite sustain the feeling. It slithered through her fingers like sand, until she was left clutching her fear and trepidation once more.

He shrugged, as though her observation was neither here nor there. Mere words.

His eyes were watchful now, though. She could sense him focusing every ounce of his attention on her, and it was debilitating.

'Perhaps, I thought, you'd been hit harder than you had anticipated, and you felt that your only move would be to get out of the company, to escape from my orbit. But that made no sense either. Because we could go for the next few years and not see one another, couldn't we? It's hardly as though we work under the same roof, in the same building.' He was leaning forward now, and his energy was so intense that she could feel it wrap itself around her like a vice.

'I don't know where this is taking us!' she said, springing to her feet. Panic had swept through her, turning her words into staccato bursts. 'Whatever my reasons for leaving, they're none of your business!'

'Sit back down,' he said with deadly quietness. 'Now!' His command cracked through the air like a whiplash, and she sank back into the chair, heart racing.

'I'm about to say something and if I'm wrong, then I'll walk out of that door and that will be the last you ever see of me again. But I've considered all the options, and I think the reason you've handed in your notice affects me quite a bit.'

Jessica swallowed painfully, aware that her mouth was dry.

'I have no idea what you're getting at,' she said bravely. 'And I think that it's time you left. I've quit and that's all there is to it. You can't force an explanation out of me, and you can't force me to go back to work for you.'

'You're pregnant, aren't you?'

It was a question, but posed as a statement, and the blood rushed to her head like a tidal wave, suddenly freed from all constraints. She found that she couldn't speak, couldn't think. The drumbeat in her ears was too loud, and even as she maintained her horrified silence she knew that it pronounced the truth of what he had just said.

She should have rushed in to defend herself, cried out in amused denial, anything but sit there in silence.

'Don't be ridiculous.' Her voice was barely above a whisper, and unsteady. Her hands, clasped on her lap, were shaking, and she quickly stuck them under her thighs, sitting on them.

'Why don't you save us forty minutes of pointless discussion on the subject, and just admit it? You're leaving because you're carrying my baby.' He raked his fingers through his hair and stood up, as though the words had generated a level of energy in him that had to be worked off.

He began pacing the room and she followed him with her eyes.

'And did you have any intention of telling me?' he asked grimly, walking over to her and leaning over her, his hands on either side of her arm rests, so that she was compelled to push herself into the chair.

'Please go.'

'I'm not leaving this house until you tell me the truth!' The words sliced through the air like a knife.

'It's true. I'm pregnant.' There was nothing to be gained by lying. She might get rid of him temporarily, but she knew that he would return, over and over, waiting to see her swelling stomach, waiting to see his accusations verified. And she could hardly move house in an attempt to escape him, could she?

'I thought...'

'That it was the perfect ploy to find yourself a husband?' he sneered, and she flung her head back, shocked and furious at where his thinking was carrying him.

'How dare you...?'

'How dare I what...Jessica? Push you into a corner?'

'Get out!'

'Or else what? You'll throw me out? Hardly.' He laughed coldly, and she struggled to match this ice-cold stranger in front of her with the sensuous, witty man who had made her laugh and made love to her, and changed the course of her life.

He was still looming over her, so close that his face was almost touching hers. 'Was that the plan? A carefully orchestrated weekend of lovemaking, with just enough protests about independence to stave off any worries I might have had about your becoming clingy, and a pregnancy at the end of it? Pregnancy and marriage? Was that the idea, Jessica?' His voice had grown steadily harsher, and as she looked at him in horror she could feel herself breathing quickly.

'You're mad,' she finally whispered. 'How could you imagine for a minute that I *planned* this pregnancy?' She gave a bitter, shallow laugh.

He couldn't have been further from the truth. She closed her eyes and relived that weak, collapsing feeling as she had stood in her bathroom and stared as two blue lines had appeared in their little windows on that tester. She couldn't begin to explain the emotion that had swept over her, but at no time had she felt the slightest inclination to tell him what had happened. From the start she had seen it as uniquely *her* problem.

'Are you denying it?'

'Does it matter one way or the other? You're going to believe what you want, anyway.'

'Answer me! Dammit!'

She almost expected him to get hold of her and shake her, but his hands remained gripping the sides of the chair, his white knuckles a testimony to what he was feeling. Fury, she guessed, suddenly weary with the whole thing. His mind was probably working overtime as well at the thought of how he could wriggle out of the situation. As far as she was concerned, he had nothing to worry about on that score.

'You're a sick man if you think that I would get myself pregnant for the sole purpose of trapping you into marriage. I made a mistake, it's as simple as that. I calculated that I wouldn't be in a fertile period, and my calculations were wrong, probably only by a couple of days, but a miss is as good as a mile in this instance, isn't it?' His breath fanned her face and she had to steel herself to meet his eyes. 'I know you think there's a huge female contingent out there, gasping for the privilege of trapping you into marriage, but I'm not one of them. Whether you believe me or not is up to you. I'm sorry you found out—'

'Because, fired as you are with moral ethics, you had no intention of telling me.' His mouth twisted angrily, and she flinched.

'This is *my* problem,' she said fiercely.

'And nothing whatsoever to do with me?'

'That's right!'

'An Immaculate Conception. The Pope would be interested.'

'You know what I mean.'

'Explain it to me, why don't you?'

'I don't understand you,' Jessica muttered. 'One minute you're raging at me because you think I'm a conniving gold-digger. The next minute, you're raging at me because you think I'm not.' Their eyes met and she held his narrowed stare, even though it was hard.

She was the first to look down, and it was a relief when he pushed himself away from the chair and went to sit on the sofa.

'You made it quite clear what sort of man you are,' she said, pausing in between her words to harness her thoughts into some semblance of order. 'Fast lane with work, fast lane with women. Wasn't one of your complaints that your last girlfriend was getting a little too cosy for your liking?' She stared mutinously at him, daring him to contradict her, but he remained silent. 'I respect that. The last thing I intended to do was push you into a corner, force you into premature responsibility with someone you barely know.'

'So your plan was…what? Exactly?'

'To cope on my own,' she told him. 'Isn't that obvious?'

'And coping on your own starts by your handing in your notice, thereby cutting off your income.'

'I had no choice,' Jessica said through gritted teeth.

'So now you have no job...what then?'

'I intend to find another job.'

'Doing what?'

'The same sort of thing I was doing before,' she snapped tensely.

'Oh, but correct me if I'm wrong. Permanent jobs are a bit thin on the ground for women who are pregnant, aren't they? Don't employers look askance at women who will only be available for work for a matter of a few months?'

'Temp work, then,' she said uncomfortably.

'Does that pay well?'

'I'm sure I could find something...' Her voice dwindled off and she stared down at her fingers, frowning.

'Filing? Typing? Temp workers get the dregs of the work and they're paid relatively little. A pittance when you consider that you intended to cover some substantial costs. Of course, you might have a large amount of savings stashed away somewhere, for just such a rainy day as this...'

'I could make do...'

'Without money and without family support...'

Jessica glared at him, wishing that she had never let slip confidences which were now being used against her.

'I can manage.'

'And your problems don't cease with the birth of the baby, do they?' he carried on relentlessly. She could feel tears gathering in the corners of her eyes and she blinked them away. 'You'll have to get your act together and find yourself a damn good job once the baby's born if you're to cover the costs of what...childcare? Nursery? And all that on your own.'

'Are you suggesting that I...terminate this pregnancy?'

She could barely form the words. The thought of doing any such thing disgusted her and if that was the route he was heading down, then he could walk right out of that door and carry on walking.

Not once had she contemplated an abortion. Her initial response had been one of confusion and fear, but she couldn't deny that from the start she had also felt a certain wild thrill at the thought of bringing a baby into the world. It hadn't been part of her plan, but she wanted this baby with an intensity she would never have thought possible. So much for the biological clock she had always assumed she didn't have.

'You insult me,' he told her with freezing disdain. 'I would no more think of suggesting such a thing than I would advise you to jump off a cliff.' He paused and appeared to turn his thoughts over in his head, like someone swilling a mouthful of fine wine, tasting, rolling it over on his tongue.

Eventually he said, 'So we've agreed that bringing up a baby on your own is as good as impossible.'

'We agree on no such thing! Thousands of women do it and cope quite satisfactorily.' She would never have admitted it, but he had managed to shake some of her self-confidence. She knew that she had deliberately adopted a rosy view of what lay ahead, more as a method of self-defence than anything else, but he had forced her to stare at all the pitfalls, and she hadn't liked what she had seen.

'In most cases because they have no choice.'

'And I do?'

'Oh, yes,' he said softly. 'You most certainly do.'

She didn't like the look in his eyes. It unsettled her.

'And what's my choice?' she heard herself ask, even though she knew that the answer to the question was not something she wanted to hear.

'You marry me.'

Jessica stared at him, open-mouthed. 'Marry?' she asked, on the verge of hysterical laughter. 'You?' She couldn't help it. She could feel the laughter rising out of her stomach. Her mouth began to twitch, and the more she acknowledged that that would be an unacceptable reaction, the less capable she felt of controlling the urge.

She began to giggle, and then a flood of emotion took over. All the confusion and stress and uncertainty seemed finally to find an outlet, and she heard herself laughing. Laughing until she thought she would never stop. Laughing until the tears came to her eyes, but somehow she knew that the tears were not of jollity, but stemmed from something else.

When he slammed his fist down on the table, the noise was so loud and so incongruous that she jumped back with a gasp.

'Stop it! Now!'

'I can't help it. I'm laughing at your ridiculous suggestion.'

'You're laughing because you know that if you don't you'll crack up,' he told her grimly.

Jessica looked at him dumbly. He was right. She could feel tears of anxiety and worry begin to collect in the corner of her eyes and she glared at him with savage resentment. She had managed to build a little cocoon for herself and along he had come and destroyed it in one fell swoop.

'You're going to marry me because you have no real choice in the matter.'

'How dare you...?'

'I have no intention of relinquishing my responsibility, nor do I intend to politely knock on your door once a week on a Saturday, so that I can see my child. I hadn't banked on fatherhood, you're damned right about that, but fatherhood has managed to come along and find me and I have every intention of doing my duty.'

'Doing your duty…? This is the twentieth century!'

'No child of mine is going to grow up a bastard,' he said quietly, and Jessica flushed.

'You ought to hear yourself, Bruno Carr! You sound positively medieval! Well, we're not in the Middle Ages now, and I'll be damned if I'm going to marry you just because you say so!'

'I could make life very difficult for you, Jessica…'

'How?'

'Jobs, for a start.' He stood up and began pacing the room, pausing every so often to inspect something, even though she knew that his mind was utterly focused on what he was saying. 'My connections are widespread,' he said casually, as though discussing how many pairs of socks he possessed. 'I know everyone. Word gets around…'

'You wouldn't dare! You would never jeopardise your own child's financial future by jeopardising my earning power. That makes no sense at all.' She was barely moved by this threat because she knew that it was empty. What frightened her was the motivation behind it. Bruno Carr did not relinquish what he felt belonged to him, and this child would belong to him.

He paused and turned to face her, his eyes narrowed. 'You can't win on this, Jessica.'

'I won't marry you for the wrong reasons! It would be unfair on us both, and on the child! Can't you see that?'

'All I see is a very selfish woman who would sacrifice her child's life for the sake of her own.'

'How can you say that? How can you imply that…?'

'You would rather scrimp and save and go without than marry me? And tell me, how do you think our child will feel about that when he's old enough to understand—?'

He had managed to hit her on a vulnerable spot, and one which she had never considered.

'Aside from closing the door on any possible future you might have, you'd merrily close the door on a child's future as well. For what? To hang on to your independence?'

'There's nothing wrong with that...' she protested, but her voice had weakened.

'Absolutely nothing...when you are the only one involved.'

'But you don't love me...' she said, horrified at the desperate tone that had crept into her voice.

'Who's talking about love? We're talking about an arrangement. A business arrangement, so to speak... You've said often enough that romance is not for you. Well, I'm offering the perfect solution.'

'I can't...'

'Oh, you can,' he said silkily, his eyes steel, 'and you will. Believe me, you will.'

# CHAPTER EIGHT

BRUNO CARR always got what he wanted. Hadn't he mentioned that to Jessica in passing somewhere along the line? She should have paid a bit more attention. She certainly should never have allowed a weekend's worth of charm to blind her to the man she had glimpsed at their very first meeting. A man who expected the world to dance to his tune.

Two days ago he had left her in a state of confusion and now, as she arranged herself in suitable clothes to meet him at a restaurant in Covent Garden, she stared glumly at her reflection in the mirror.

Her stomach was still flat, showing no indication of what lay ahead.

She still hadn't worked up the courage to telephone her mother and let her know of these latest, overwhelming developments in her life. Similarly, she had put her friends on hold, unable to face the barrage of questions that would greet her announcement. They had all cheerfully given up on her and the institution of marriage.

They would have to iron out the details of their little arrangement, he had informed her. As though her life, from now on, were nothing more than a piece of cloth, to be pulled and stretched and straightened into whatever shape he desired.

I can't imagine why you're not enamoured of the idea, he had told her coldly. Wasn't an arranged marriage the ultimate in control? She had heard his words, and watched his mouth as he formed them, and had felt anything but in control. Her life had never seemed so wildly disordered and unpredictable.

She sighed and ran her fingers through her hair, sectioning it off into three, and absent-mindedly plaiting it in one long, thick braid down her back.

She knew, somewhere, that a part of her was being unreasonable.

After all, she had felt shock at the discovery of her pregnancy, but the shock had soon been replaced by a certain nervous elation. So why did something less significant fill her with such terror?

With absolutely no time to spare, she made it to the restaurant, to find him sitting on the far side with a drink in front of him.

'I wondered whether you'd chickened out of meeting me,' were his first words, though with no smile to accompany them.

'And if I had?'

She sat down, pulling the chair towards the table, and then relaxed back with her arms folded, in the classic pose of self-defence.

'Oh, I would have come and found you. And just in case the thought of running away ever crosses your mind, forget it. There would be no rock I would leave unturned to get you.'

'To get your baby, you mean,' she said bitterly.

'I stand corrected.' He gestured to the waiter for two menus, and she grabbed a few minutes' reprieve from looking at him by concentrating on the jumble of words in front of her. Salmon, steak, sauces and parcels of vegetables, whatever. She couldn't care less what she ate. A hearty appetite and the presence of Bruno Carr were two things that did not go together. Not now.

'You haven't put on much weight,' he said, settling back in his seat.

'Is that remark intended to put me at ease?'

'Is that what I'm supposed to do? Put you at ease?'

'No, of course it isn't,' Jessica said acidly. 'Marriages are best conducted in a state of cold war.'

She fiddled with the stem of her wineglass and missed the glimmer of a smile that tugged the corners of his mouth for a few seconds.

'So I take it that you've resigned yourself to the prospect...' He waited until a glass of wine had been placed in front of him and a glass of orange juice in front of her, and then leaned slightly forward. 'There's a lot to be sorted out.'

'You're a cold-hearted bastard, aren't you?' she answered.

'On the contrary,' he said smoothly. 'If I were a cold-hearted bastard, I would have allowed you to handle the entire thing on your own, as you had stupidly planned to do. The fact is, whether you like it or not, I have no intention of relinquishing my responsibility and I also have no intention of lurking on the sidelines, watching any child of mine grow up without my input. As I've told you before.'

'So you have.'

'Why aren't you looking pregnant?'

'What are you trying to say, Bruno? That you doubt me? That you think I've made the whole thing up?'

'Don't be ridiculous.' He flushed and looked away uncomfortably. 'I'm asking if you're all right. Physically, I mean. Things doing what they should be doing?' He looked at her briefly from under his lashes, and she was momentarily thrown by that glimmer of boyish charm that had captivated her.

'"Things doing what they should be doing?"' She raised

her eyebrows expressively. 'What a medically oriented question. Don't you know anything about pregnancy?'

'Well, having just been pregnant the one time...'

Jessica felt a sudden urge to smile and clicked her tongue with irritation instead. After all the defensive, hostile feelings he had recently aroused in her, she was stupefied that she could suddenly find anything he said remotely amusing. It wouldn't do, she told herself sternly. It wouldn't do at all. She couldn't let herself forget that, beneath any charm, this man would do whatever he wanted to get his own way. He would marry her for the sake of the baby and then what? Lifelong fidelity? Hardly. He didn't love her and it would simply be a matter of time before his sexual urges took him to newer hunting grounds. Because he occasionally had the knack of making her laugh meant nothing. It certainly didn't mean that a union between them wouldn't be a union on paper only.

'I doubt I'll show for another few weeks or so.' Her cheeks were burning and it was a relief when the food came and she had a chance to catch her breath.

'But you've been to the doctor...had checks...I mean, whatever checks you should have had...'

'Quite soon, but not just yet,' she informed him.

'Oh.' He appeared to digest this piece of information. 'Then how do you know...?'

'Bruno.' Jessica looked at him firmly. 'Pregnancy is a natural occurrence. I feel well enough, apart from the odd bout of morning sickness and that's on its way out. I'm sure everything is all right. There's absolutely nothing to worry about.'

'Who ever said anything about worrying?' He stabbed a piece of fish with his fork and treated her to a watered-down version of a glare.

Why did he have to be so damned *cute*? she thought

irritably. Why couldn't he be cold and detached all the time? *Cute* undermined her. His *mood swings* undermined her.

She felt a sudden gust of misery sweep over her. It was all such a parody of what should have been.

'You brought me here to discuss arrangements...' she reminded him unsteadily.

'Arrangements. Yes.' He seemed as relieved as she was to find their conversational footing back to where it should be. 'There's no need, first of all, for you to continue working out your notice.'

'You mean I can continue working until I'm ready to...have the baby?' Now that he knew the reasons for her resignation, there seemed no point in resigning after all. She knew that she would have to tell everyone at the office that she was getting married, having a baby, and that Bruno Carr was the man responsible, and she knew that there would be a buzz of gossip for a while after. But gossip died eventually. And she wasn't afraid of gossip. They were a good bunch of people, and after the initial shock and 'who'd have thought it?' remarks, they would accept it.

'I mean,' Bruno said patiently, 'you can leave immediately, *without* bothering to work out your notice at all.'

'And do what?' She looked at him questioningly, as though he had suddenly started talking a different language.

'Do nothing. Relax. Put your feet up. Plan a nursery. Whatever,' he finished irritably, watching her face.

'I intend to do no such thing,' Jessica informed him flatly. If there were one or two things to be ironed out, then they had hit the first major crease. 'I'm not going to *sit around doing nothing.* I'd go mad.'

'Lots of women do it,' he said impatiently. 'And there's no *financial* need for you to work. As my wife, you'll have whatever you need, and whenever you need it.'

Which, she thought, brought them swiftly to crease number two.

'Look, let's get one or two things straight here.' She abandoned her attempts to enjoy what remained of the food in front of her, and closed her knife and fork. 'I *am not* going to be giving up work from now and sitting around on my butt doing nothing, just because you think it might be a good idea. I am going to carry on where I am and when the time comes I shall have the baby and then go back out to work. I have no intention of becoming a financial burden to you.'

'Oh, for God's sake, woman—'

'And furthermore, while we're on the subject of money, I intend to keep my flat and rent it out.'

'As a bolt-hole?'

'As a source of income!'

'You *don't need* a source of income!'

'Nor do you, any longer!' she retorted. 'But that doesn't mean that you intend to pack in your job and sit around building shelves and doing the garden!'

They stared at one another and finally he expelled a long, frustrated sigh.

'It's a lousy idea. Pregnant women need to rest.'

'According to a man who freely admits he knows nothing whatsoever on the subject!'

'Lord, give me strength...' he muttered under his breath.

'If you're beginning to regret your little proposition,' she said hopefully, 'then now's the time to retract it.' If she was going to go along with this so-called business arrangement, then she intended to lay down a few ground rules before she found herself swept up into a world in which she had no say. There was no way on the face of the earth that she would follow in her mother's footsteps and become the silent partner in an unfair dictatorship.

She thrust out her chin belligerently, and he looked at her with a shadow of amusement.

'I wouldn't dream of doing any such thing.'

She noticed that he had similarly closed his knife and fork, and she wondered whether this blast of reality had affected his appetite as well. If it had, then all the better.

'Now, the wedding...' he began.

'*Business arrangement*, you mean?'

'Pick your choice of words. The sooner the better as far as I'm concerned.'

'Why?'

She felt a nervous flutter in her stomach at the prospect of fixing a date, but her expression remained unchanged.

'Wouldn't you like to become accustomed to *our* home before the baby comes along?'

No, she was tempted to say. She thought of sharing a home with him and was attacked by another queasy sense of anxiety.

'Oh, getting accustomed to some bricks and mortar doesn't take very long,' she said with conviction. If only, she thought, she didn't feel something for him. She wasn't too sure what she felt, but she could sense it there, deep inside, for ever stirring. A business arrangement involved two dispassionate strangers, but they weren't, were they?

'Stop being so damned obstructive. It won't work.'

'What won't work?'

'Trying to put off the inevitable.' He signalled for some coffee. 'And I don't want you getting cold feet at the last minute. We both know what the outcome is going to be and you might as well face the facts.' He sipped some of his coffee and regarded her calmly over the rim of the cup.

Those eyes. Those fingers curled around the handle of the cup. However much she tried to persuade herself that she found him unreasonable, lacking in the milk of human tenderness and ruthless to the core, her body still responded with eagerness at the mere sight of him. Why? *Why? Why?*

'So we've agreed that I continue working until the time comes.'

'I can hardly drag you to my house and chain you to a piece of furniture.'

'So you won't pass the word down that my employment with your company is terminated.'

'Sir.'

'I beg your pardon?'

'You sound as though you should be adding *Sir* to the end of that question. For God's sake, can't you relax a bit about this whole thing?'

'How do you expect me to do that?' she almost shrieked. 'I feel as though I'm on a roller coaster all of a sudden. How easy is it to relax on a roller coaster?' She looked at her coffee with distaste.

'Life is going to change for the both of us,' he said coolly. 'You're not the only one who's going to be feeling the repercussions of this, are you?' He called for the bill, but kept watching her, as though half expecting her to make a sudden dash for the door.

'I can take the underground back to my place,' she said, once he had paid.

'We're going back to my house.' He steered her towards a taxi and she helplessly allowed herself to be ushered in.

'What for?'

'Because I say so.'

'You're not my lord and master,' she protested grimly under her breath.

'If you want to be involved in joint decision making, then you're going to have to act in a more mature manner. Circumstance has put us both in a situation we hadn't banked on, and now that we're here we might just as well make the best of it.'

'That's easier said than done!'

'Only if you don't wake up to reality.' He looked at her with steely-eyed hardness. 'You can either make things difficult for yourself, or else you can accept the situation we're both in and enjoy it.'

'"Enjoy it?"' she asked incredulously. 'Are you *enjoying it*? Are you looking forward to marrying someone you'd rather not marry? Does your heart thrill at the prospect of sharing a house with a woman who was meant to be a temporary blip?' Just uttering the words brought on an attack of self-pity, and she turned away and glared out of the window.

Her hormones were up the spout. Every word he had spoken was true and she knew that if a friend had come to her with a tale of pregnancy and marriage to a man whom most women would give their eye-teeth to have, her advice would have been to take it in her stride and enjoy it. She would have said that things could have been a whole lot worse. She would have counselled her friend to see the best in a man who was prepared to adopt the mantle of responsibility when he had no need to. Such men were few and far between.

It wasn't even as if she had nurtured romantic notions of white weddings with fairy-tale endings. This marriage of convenience was a logical step in a logical life, and as such she should have embraced it wholeheartedly.

So why couldn't she?

She wasn't going to make things easier for herself if she insisted on fighting him every step of the way.

The taxi drew up in front of his house and she looked at it curiously. She had pictured him as a man who lived in a penthouse suite at the top of an exclusive block of apartments somewhere very central. She couldn't have been further from the truth. His house was set back in gardens in a quiet street in the St John's Wood area, and as they entered it she was struck by a feeling of cosiness. It was no sprawling mansion, but neither was it a box. Warm, red brick, ivy clambering to touch the window-panes, and inside rich, deep colours and furniture that was old and comfortable.

'I thought all top businessmen who lived on their own inhabited apartments with lots of chrome and black,' she said eventually, gazing at the paintings on the walls and trying to place a couple of them.

'Yet another of your hare-brained notions.' He led the way to the sitting room, which was small and had, a rarity in London, a wonderful fireplace with the original tiles on it. On the wall above the fire was an exquisite mirror, and, flanking either side, two paintings that looked disturbingly familiar. Everything she had seen spoke of wealth, but wealth without any accompanying fanfare.

'The house has been in my family for generations,' he said, following her gaze and picking up on her surprise at her surroundings.

'It's...'

'A far cry from chrome and black?'

'Absolutely splendid.'

'Well, that's hurdle number one over,' he said dryly. 'Would you like something to drink? Tea? Coffee?'

'Tea would be fine, thank you. Milk, one sugar.' There were so many basic things he didn't know about her, and yet, every so often, she was struck by the strangest feeling that she had known this man for ever. She sat down in the sitting room, waiting for him to return, and thought that they should be writing down their CVs for each other to read. Filling in all the gaps which were normally filled in between two people during the period of courtship, when they got to know one another. They were doing things the wrong way around. The baby before the marriage and the marriage before the relationship. The scope for things going horrendously wrong was so enormous that she couldn't even dwell on it.

The most she knew she could hope for was the thing he saw as perfectly acceptable. That they would have the baby and would be able to communicate without friction. With no love to confuse the issue, their relationship would never soar to any great heights, but they might eventually become friends. Two friends sharing a house. She would turn a blind eye to his sexual adventures elsewhere, and presumably he would turn a blind eye to hers.

Not, she knew, that she would have any.

She had never considered marriage, but now that she was being forced to she might just as well face facts. She was no twentieth-century woman who carried the torch for sexual freedom, whether there was a ring on her finger or not.

For her, marriage was a commitment.

She stared blindly through the bay window at the glimpse of sky and garden outside.

It was all about love.

All about being in love.

Her mind began to travel back down the past few months, but this time all the connections were made. It was as though she was seeing her life, for the first time ever, with absolute clarity.

She had proudly thought that her background had hardened her, turned any thoughts of romance into cynicism. She had managed to convince herself for years that her career was all she wanted out of life. She had seen it as a positive sign, the fact that her relationships had been brief and pain-free. Men, she had thought, were objects of desire or at least temporary enjoyment.

She could see where her thoughts were taking her, and was powerless to drag them away from the route.

Outside, the sky was blue and flawless, undisturbed by clouds. It made the perfect canvas against which to view her life and to see how willingly she had succumbed to her illusions of independence and freedom from the rest of the human race.

The truth was that she had just never found love. Until Bruno Carr had arrived on the scene. All those intense, conflicting emotions she had felt in his presence had nothing to do with dislike. They had to do with opening her eyes for the first time in her life, and taking her first stretch, and finally coming alive. It was a shock in much the same way, she supposed, that a new-born baby feels the shock of taking its first breath.

She could feel her breath getting ragged, but she continued staring in an unfocused manner through the window, carried along with her thoughts like a stick floating randomly on an ocean tide.

When had she fallen? Impossible to tell, but fallen she had. Well and truly fallen in love with him. Little wonder that the pregnancy had caused her no real grief. Subconsciously, she had wanted his baby from the start. She closed her eyes to try and block out her thoughts, but they kept on rolling. She felt sick.

She didn't hear him enter the room. The first she knew of his presence was when he asked her if she felt all right.

'You're as white as a sheet.'

She opened her eyes and looked at him, and she felt as if she were seeing him for the first time. She accepted her cup of tea and blew gently on the surface, then watched in silence as he sat down opposite her and crossed his legs.

This terrible realisation would have to be her secret. She would be businesslike and calm because that was the only way to conduct herself without revealing what was inside her.

He was looking at her, waiting for some kind of response, and she took a deep breath.

'Just some passing nausea. My stomach hasn't been accustomed to rich food.' She hazarded a smile which met with a frown. 'How long have you lived here?' she asked politely, reaching for the first pointless remark she could think of, and his frown deepened.

'I've already told you. The house has been in—'

'Your family for generations. Of course. Forgot.'

'What's the matter with you?' He narrowed his eyes, searching to get inside her head, and she met his stare blandly.

'Amnesia and pregnancy. Well documented,' she told him. She sipped some tea and adopted a more relaxed pose.

'I don't think we should rush into the marriage thing,' she said. 'The baby's not due for another few months. I think we should take the time to at least get to know one another a bit.' She would need the time to let her emotions settle a little, or at least to learn to control them. The thought of sharing his house immediately filled her with horror.

'Actually, I think we know each other better than you imagine,' he remarked. 'But if you want to wait a couple of months as opposed to a couple of weeks, then that's fine by me. I take it you won't object to an engagement ring.'

'Do people still get engaged these days?' She knew that they did, but an engagement seemed almost a greater show of hypocrisy than the prospect of marriage. Engagements, she thought, were all about being wrapped up in dreams and hope and plans. Rings to be shown off as the glowing proof of love.

'I have no idea…' he shrugged '…and it's not something

that I care about one way or another. But my mother would find it very disturbing if the conventional rites of passage weren't adhered to. The gesture might mean nothing to either of us, but it would mean a great deal to her.'

His words stabbed into her with the precision of a sharp knife, but she forced herself to smile.

'In that case...' she shrugged as well '...it doesn't matter to me one way or the other, as you say, and if it would make your mother happier, then that's fine.' Things should have been different. They should have been planning a life of happiness, with a baby on the way. But maybe it was better like this. If there were no dreams, then there were no dreams to be shattered.

'Come on,' he said abruptly, standing up. 'You might as well have the guided tour of the place.'

'Why not?'

She followed him into all the downstairs rooms, and murmured favourably, and tried to close her eyes to thoughts of them happily growing old together, sitting on the sofa side by side, sharing laughter in the kitchen, entertaining friends in the dining room.

When they went upstairs, the beating of her heart quickened. Behind the closed doors lay bedrooms and the thought of bedrooms brought her out in a cold sweat.

The layout of the upstairs mirrored that of downstairs, with a large, central hall off which the rooms fell. Four huge bedrooms and a large sitting room which had been turned into a television area. Somehow, she couldn't imagine Bruno Carr finding the time to sit in front of a TV, but she refrained from saying that. Instead, she commented on the furnishings, peering at the paintings and delaying the onset of a further attack of nerves when confronted with the bedroom. His bedroom. Their bedroom. Their bed. God, would he want to touch her? Or would his eyes glaze over with disinterest?

His bedroom, as it turned out, was large enough to include a sitting area, in addition to a massive *en suite* bathroom.

'Big,' Jessica said weakly, not straying from the door.

'What the hell is wrong with you?' He swung around and stood in front of her, propping himself up with his hands on either side of the doorway.

'Nothing's wrong with me.' She licked her lips nervously.

'Does the thought of sharing a house with me frighten you?' he asked, reading her mind, and she shook her head vigorously.

'Shall we move on?'

'Not until you answer a few questions.' He pulled her inside the bedroom, towards the small, squashy sofa by the bay window, and she reluctantly sat down, averting her eyes from the king-size Victorian bed dominating the room.

How many women had he shared that bed with?

The question brought a surge of angry, jealous colour to her face.

'Ever since you walked through the front door, you've been acting like a zombie. Why?' It was less of a question and more of a demand for information. He was still standing over her, hands thrust into his pockets, but now he sat down next to her on the sofa, his thighs splayed against her own.

'It all seems unreal,' Jessica mumbled, inclining her body to look at him, and feeling the full force of his personality like a sledgehammer.

She knew every line on his face, the way his mouth curved when he smiled and became a thin line when he was angry. It amazed her that she had never sought to discover why it was that a man she had told herself meant nothing to her could still have become so familiar. How had she not added up all the signs before? How could love have overcome her so stealthily that she had been unaware of herself falling headlong into the ambush?

'What do you imagine life will be like once we're married? Once you've taken up residence here and there's no flat to run to?' His velvety voice seemed to reach her from a great distance and it was an effort to keep her eyes on his face with some semblance of normality.

'I don't know.' A shrug. 'Guess I'll have to wait and see. My mind will be on the pregnancy, anyway. And after that...well, babies require a lot of attention.'

'Which still hasn't answered my question.'

'What answer do you want?' she replied hotly. She resented his composure. She knew that he found all this much easier to deal with because the prospect of marriage didn't threaten him. He could quite happily cohabit with her because she meant nothing to him emotionally and so would never really disturb his lifestyle.

Quite honestly, she could have hurled something very big and very heavy at him.

'The goddamn truth!'

'No, you don't!' she snapped, close to tears now. 'The truth is the last thing you want! What you want is my total agreement with everything you say! You want me to nod my head all the time and tell you what a clever person you are!'

'You're talking absolute rubbish!'

She was leaning towards him, their faces almost touching, and through all her rage and misery she still felt a yearning to close her eyes and put her mouth against his. She still wanted his hands to slip beneath her shirt and caress her swollen breasts.

'No, I'm not, Bruno! Let's look at things dispassionately, shall we? I was good enough for a weekend, but that was all you were interested in...'

'If I recall, that was *your* point of view,' he grated.

'Okay, then! A weekend, a week, maybe a month but then I got pregnant and, now that you've found out, you've decided to launch yourself into fatherhood and wrap the whole business up with a phoney marriage, which means nothing to you...'

'And you want it to...?'

'I never said that!'

'Then what precisely *are* you saying?'

'I'm saying...' She miserably tried to work out an answer to his question. The only thing revolving in her brain was the hideous revelation that she loved this man and that her love wasn't reciprocated. What kind of answer could she give him? 'Oh, I don't know.' She buried her head in her hands, and was giving herself a strong lecture on self-control when she felt his hand against the nape of her neck, massaging it.

'Turn around,' he said roughly, and she obeyed, flexing her muscles, then allowing her head to drop. She didn't want to think and his hands on her neck were so soothing. His thumbs pressed against her bones, rotating along her shoulders, and she sighed with pleasure.

'Like it?' he murmured, and she nodded. His fingers found her shoulder blades, then her spine, pushing against the line of vertebrae, and she involuntarily gave a stifled moan of satisfaction.

His hands circled around to her ribcage, then back to her spine, then beneath her breasts and she gave a little gasp.

'You're bloody tense,' he said softly, his breath tickling her ear. 'I'm no masseur, and I can feel it. Just relax.' He unclasped her bra and spanned his hands across her back, gently pressing and kneading her flesh.

'I'm not tense.'

'And stop arguing. You argue too much.' He circled her waist with his hands, then rolled them up higher until his fingers lay provocatively beneath her breasts, fuller and heavier with the pregnancy.

With eyes still closed, Jessica leaned back against him, tilting her head over his shoulder, and shuddered as she felt him cup her breasts, then slowly he began to massage them. She sank deeper into him, and when he shifted slightly she lay fully back, her body still arched up to him, her head inclined over the arm of the sofa.

She felt as though the past few weeks had been spent in a state of constant need, a craving that she had refused to acknowledge.

He leant over her and his tongue flicked against her nipples. The moan that escaped her lips seemed to come from someone else. It was a moan of the deepest contentment. His mouth covered her nipple, then he was suckling on it and she squirmed and smiled and curled her fingers into his hair.

Between her legs grew damp and she spread them apart, knowing that his hand would find the hungry moistness beneath her lacy briefs. Her skirt had hitched up to her thighs and he began to stroke the inside of them, while he continued to lick and play with her breasts with his mouth.

'See. Don't be afraid. Marriage won't be nearly as bad as you anticipate.'

His words took a second to sink in, but as soon as they did her brain seemed to go into overdrive, analysing what he had said, dissecting every hidden nuance.

The thought of living with Bruno, married to him, having to conceal her love like a dirty secret, offered enough of a prospect of lifelong hurt. But to have him touch her, knowing that he didn't love her, knowing, in due course, that he probably touched other women as well, would be beyond endurance.

persuade her to keep him. But to have him touch her, knowing that he didn't love her, knowing, in fact, that to touch
her would be beyond
endurance.

# CHAPTER NINE

THE shock of opening her eyes and seeing Bruno staring
down at her, white-faced, was almost enough to make
Jessica want to slip back into unconsciousness.

Then, hard on the heels of that, she remembered the se-
quence of events that had brought her to a hospital, and
she struggled to sit up.

'The baby.' She knew that she was bleeding. She could
feel it and a flood of sudden panic gripped her. She had
lost the baby. She just knew it. She hadn't realised how
desperately she had wanted this baby until now. 'How long
have I been here?' Her voice was unsteady and she glanced
around her with an expression of fear. White walls had
never seemed more intimidating. She was in a gown. One
of those hideous hospital gowns that automatically brought
on an attack of malaise the second they were put on.

'Minutes. Do you remember what happened?' She hardly
recognised his voice. Gone was the composure and authority. She looked more carefully at him and saw lines of
anxiety and tension around his eyes.

'I ran into the road.' She shook her head and made no
effort to stop the trickle of tears that ran down her face.
Very gently, he wiped them with his handkerchief.

He was already treating her like an invalid. Confirmation
enough that the pregnancy was no more.

'Don't talk about it if you feel you don't want to.'

'Was I hit?'

'The car braked just in time.' He managed a smile.
'You'd know if you'd been hit, I assure you. Speaking, you

understand, as someone with a limited medical background.'

He was humouring her, and she smiled weakly back at him, appreciating his efforts to sustain her spirits.

'You came here by ambulance,' he continued. His voice was like a soothing balm. Just what she needed. She remembered his hands massaging her back. That had been just what she had needed as well. She squeezed her eyes shut for a few seconds to block out the image and then opened them and looked at him.

Now, of course, there would be no wedding. There would be no need to get married, and she felt a spreading void begin to wash over her. No wedding, no baby, no more Bruno Carr. She had been so terrified of marrying him and involving herself in a life of loving from the sidelines, but now the thought of never seeing him again filled her with a different type of terror. It was like staring into a black hole.

'Actually, you more or less came to on the way here. You've only been in the room for a short while.' He took one of her hands between his, and was it her imagination or could she feel the pity oozing out of him? 'The nurse will be back in a few minutes. You've already been examined by a doctor, and they'll be taking you to be scanned to see...' He didn't end the sentence, but there was no need for him to. She knew what he meant.

'What did the doctor say?'

'There's a heartbeat, but...'

'That might not last, might it? I might be heading for a miscarriage. Well, after all that...' She tried to laugh but couldn't and he didn't say anything.

It threatened to become a silence filled with dangerously raw feelings of self-pity and despair, when the nurse bustled in, looking starched and cheerful. Jessica looked glumly at her and wondered how hospital employees always managed to maintain such relentless good humour.

'Radiologist's all ready for you now, my love.' She was efficiently transferred from bed to wheelchair, which made her feel even more of an invalid, and she was immeasurably grateful when Bruno took her hand in his and held it.

This, she knew, was one of the many reasons why she loved him. He was a source of strength. However often she told herself that he was autocratic and over-forceful, she knew that those were just the desperate postulations of someone who recognised qualities she would rather not acknowledge.

The short spin passed in a blur. Fear had congealed itself like a ball in her head.

The room with the scanning machine was dark and she propped herself onto the narrow bed and lay down, watching as the radiologist swivelled the screen at an angle so that she could see what was happening on it. Or not, as the case might be.

Bruno was still clasping her hand, and now he squeezed it. The radiologist, a middle-aged woman with an expression of perpetual concentration, was talking in the background. Referring to the accident. Then she switched on the machine and began to roll the monitor across Jessica's well-greased stomach.

'There,' she said, finding what she was looking for. 'There's the foetus. And there, you see, is the heart. Beating away quite merrily.'

A blob. An indistinct grey blob with a merrily beating heart. The flood of relief was so intense that Jessica felt she might possibly pass out. She listened while Bruno began asking questions, and half absorbed what the radiologist was saying about measurements and stage of development.

A merrily beating heart. She stared, fixated, at the screen, just to make sure that she could still see the beating pin-prick.

'Of course,' the radiologist said, switching off the monitor, 'you'll want to rest for a bit. Just until the bleeding settles, which should be quite soon. And then take it easy.'

'Oh, she'll be doing just that,' Jessica heard Bruno say. 'When I take her home.'

Home? Whose home?

'You can't stay in your flat on your own,' he repeated the following day as they were in the car and heading away from the hospital. 'Before you start launching into a debate on the subject. You're bloody lucky...' His voice stumbled a bit, but he carried on almost immediately in his usual tone of command. 'You heard what the woman said. You need to rest.'

'I can rest at my own place.' But it was a token protest. The fact was that she wanted to put her feet up, at least for a little while.

'Absolutely not. No way, no how, no debate,' he told her warningly, and she glanced across at him, trying to read his mind and unearth how he felt.

Relieved that everything was all right? Or disturbed that he had been given a glimpse of possible liberation from an unwanted marriage and was now forced back to square one? She daredn't ask him. The thought of what he might say by way of reply was enough to make her cringe inwardly.

'How are you feeling?' He glanced across at her. This was the third time he had asked that question.

'Still shaken, but all right. Why do you keep asking?'

'Why do you think?' He let the rhetorical question hang in the air and then evidently gave up on her saying any-

thing. 'You could say that I was responsible for everything
that happened, couldn't you?' he said conversationally. His
face was impassive, but there were thoughts running
through his head. She could tell from the tense set of his
jaw.

'How do you work that one out?'

'Don't be obtuse, Jessica,' he ground out. He shot her a
brief glance, then reverted his attention to the road. 'I
touched you, and you obviously didn't want to be touched,
so you fled. Without thinking.'

'Well, it's very good of you to take the blame, and I
wish I could let you get away with it, but...'

'But...?'

'My reaction had nothing to do with you,' she told him
bluntly. 'Yes, you touched me, but I allowed myself to be
touched. I just felt, when it happened, that I needed to get
away. To escape.'

'Which pretty much seems to sum up your feelings ever
since we reached the decision to get married for the sake
of the baby. Or maybe even before. You're terrified of commitment, even the sort of commitment that doesn't have the
burden of love and romance to live up to. Am I right?'

'I suppose I am,' Jessica said carefully and he expelled
a long, frustrated sigh.

'In which case, you're free.'

'What?'

'You heard me,' he said flatly, not looking at her.
'You're free. I'm not going to force you to live a life of
terror and abhorrence simply because of my principles.'

'Are you being serious?' Her ears had taken in what he
had just said, and her mind was slowly registering the fact
that, far from feeling heady with a sense of release, she felt
as though she were being sucked down a plug hole.

'I've never been more serious in my entire life,' he told

her grimly. 'I mistakenly imagined that we might have rubbed along harmoniously as a married couple for the sake of the baby, but what happened has proved that that's complete nonsense. Your aversion to me is so intense that it almost ending up endangering our child's life.'

So she had got what she had clamoured so loudly for after all. Didn't they say that you should be very careful what you wished for because wishes had a nasty habit of coming true?

'Naturally, we will have to have something drawn up by lawyers.'

'I really don't feel up to discussing this just at the moment, Bruno,' she said feebly. She rested her head against the window-pane and shut her eyes. Her ears were pounding and the trauma of her near miss was catching up on her. Or so it felt. She was very tired. All she wanted to do was get into a bed and drift off to sleep.

'You'll still be coming to stay with me for a while,' he continued, ignoring her lack of response. 'At least for a week. There's no way that your stubbornness is going to come before health.'

Jessica didn't answer. After a while, she was aware of the car slowing down, pulling up in front of the house, then she heard him open his door, and eventually she lugged herself out of the car and followed him inside.

'I'll need the key to your place,' he told her. 'I'll have to bring some of your clothes over.'

'I can always go and fetch them myself tomorrow,' she said.

'Still fighting for your independence up to the last, aren't you, Jessica?' She heard the cynicism in his voice and flinched. 'Still totally incapable of accepting even the smallest of favours just in case you might find a corner of your precious self-control eroded.'

'Please, Bruno. Not now. I'm feeling very fragile at the moment.'

She knew that he would respect that, but for how long? He was furious with her and she wondered whether that wasn't in part due to the fact that, just this once, he had found himself incapable of ordering events precisely how he wanted to.

He had wanted to marry her, had wanted to adopt the mantle of fatherhood, and now he must be seeing it slipping away from him.

How do you think *I* feel? she wanted to shout at him. She would be financially secure, she knew that, but the emptiness stretching out in front of her was almost beyond endurance.

Weekly visits. Just often enough to ensure that she never recovered from the havoc he had wreaked on her heart. And then watching from the sidelines as over time he found someone. In fact, probably not that much time before the inevitable happened. He was an intensely sexual man. Celibacy, she guessed, was not a word he was overly familiar with.

He walked her up the stairs, keeping pace with her, and then led her into one of the guest bedrooms.

'Your keys?' he reminded her, standing by the door and watching as she sank onto the bed.

'Yes, my keys.' She rustled around in her bag and unearthed them from underneath a half-empty packet of mints and an assortment of pens and stray items of make-up. Funny, with all her passion for control, she had never been able to control her bag. Was there a name for someone whose life resembled the state of their bag? 'I don't feel happy about you rummaging around in my flat—' she began.

'Tough. You've got zero choice in the matter.' He took

the keys from her and vanished. She waited a few minutes, then slowly changed into more comfortable clothes, drew the curtains and lay down on the bed.

She must have dozed off, because when she next opened her eyes evening had arrived, and Bruno was standing by the bed. On the chair by the bay window, she saw her suitcase, and she sat up, momentarily disoriented.

'How long have I been asleep?' she asked.

'Hours. I got back here and didn't want to disturb you, and I've been popping in every so often to check and make sure you were all right.'

The overhead light hadn't been switched on, so she couldn't properly make out the expression on his face, but at least his voice had no undertones of anger.

'Tea.' He nodded in the direction of the bedside table, and Jessica gratefully took the mug and drank. Warm but fortifying.

'How are you feeling?'

'Much better. Thank you.'

He pulled a chair across to the bed and sat down next to her, so that he was more on her level and she didn't have to crane her neck upwards to see him. She knew they would have to talk. They had worked out details of the marriage that wasn't to be, and now they would have to work out arrangements for her and the baby after it was born. And claiming exhaustion was an excuse that wouldn't hold water for ever.

How could she explain that marrying him and enduring the torment of her love in silence had seemed unbearable, but the alternative was even worse?

She couldn't. She had made her bed and she would now have to lie on it. Wasn't that what her mother had once said to her? That she had made her bed and would simply have to accept all that went with it? Ironic that her situation was reversed. Bitterly ironic.

'So,' he said casually, not looking at her, 'there's a baby inside you.'

'Could we turn the lights on? I can't see your face.'

'In a minute.' He relaxed back in the chair and stuck his legs out, crossing them at the ankle. 'I've never...had an experience...'

'I'm relieved to hear it,' Jessica said. 'It would be a bit off-putting to discover you'd fathered a herd of children before.'

'I doubt you'll be able to get back to work as rapidly as you had anticipated...'

She looked at his hard profile, and then found that the glance had turned into a stare.

'Possibly not,' Jessica admitted, taking advantage of his averted face to drink him in. There was an awkward pause, and she said, simply to break the silence, 'What did you pack? Perhaps I could have a shower...'

Without a word, he stood up, fetched the suitcase from the chair and deposited it on the bed next to her. His silence was beginning to rattle her. He had accepted that there would be no marriage, and now she wondered whether he had decided that he could cease to make all efforts with her. Why bother to build any kind of tenuous relationship when there was now no need? She had been reduced to being no more than the mother of his child. Once this week was over, she would return to her flat and he would visit occasionally, she guessed, to make sure that she hadn't flung herself in front of another passing car. But meanwhile he would carry on with his life and contact would only be resumed once the baby was born. By then, all legal arrangements would be in place. He would be super-efficient when it came to that.

'Are you going to be all right to manage yourself?'

'I'm not ill, Bruno. Had a slight shock, admittedly, but I'm fine.' She sat up and swung open the suitcase to find that he had packed several dresses, her entire underwear drawer, no pyjamas, one shirt and a pair of trousers which had clearly been the first pair his hands had happened to chance upon hanging in the wardrobe. Jade-green silk, appropriate only for evening wear.

Jessica tipped the suitcase upside down and stared at the contents.

'You envisage a series of cocktail parties for me over the next week, do you?'

'A series of cocktail parties?' He moved to turn on the light, which revealed the inappropriate selection in all their glory.

'Dresses?' She looked at him quizzically, momentarily forgetting her personal state of depression. 'I'm supposed to be relaxing for the next few days. Does this...' she held up a scarlet number which had not seen the light of day for years '...strike you as a relaxing outfit?'

'It's a very jolly colour,' he commented, flushing. 'Thought it might cheer you up.'

'Okay. So what was the reasoning behind the two little black affairs?'

'Those must have found their way in by mistake.' He cleared his throat and peered at the bundle on the bed. He picked one up and he held it up by one shoestring strap to the light. 'It's a very attractive number,' he said, observing it from several angles. 'It never ceases to amaze me the clothes that women somehow manage to squeeze their bodies into.' He dropped it back on the bed and folded his arms.

'That's as may be, but...' she looked at him with an inward sigh of despair '...it's not a useful lot of clothes. I

shall have to go myself and fetch some more.' She prepared
to swing her legs over the side of the bed.

'Not on your life! If you just tell me what to bring over,
then I can do it myself.'

'But I wanted to have a shower now,' Jessica said a little
plaintively.

'Fine. Stay right there. I'll be back in a second.'

He vanished, to return literally a minute later with a
short-sleeved shirt in one hand.

'Here. You can put this on.'

'But it's yours.'

He looked at it as though seeing it for the first time. 'Oh,
so it is. Well, it won't bite and it's been recently laundered.
Have a shower and I'll be back up in half an hour with
something for you to eat.' Before she could protest he was
walking out of the door, and as soon as he had vacated the
room she made her way to the bathroom, and had a shower.

The memory of the bleeding was already beginning to
fade away, and her spirits began to lift a little.

She still couldn't seem to harness her thoughts, but at
least she no longer felt on the verge of cracking up.

If she could manage to maintain her good humour, then
it would give her time to build up her defences against him.
It had worked for her in the past. She could remember,
even as a child, learning to bring the shutters down over
her eyes, to control her emotions when her father had been
in one of his moods and jeering at her school efforts had
become a form of fun. Tears had never worked then. They
had only fuelled his cruelty. But gradually she had learned
to blank out what he'd been saying and to look through
him and past him. Out towards a happier future.
Somewhere. And in time the self-imposed control had become second nature for her. She had carried it all the way

through to her adult life when it had clothed and protected her like a second skin.

This was different, but wasn't the objective more or less the same?

She slowly dried herself, brushed her hair, leaving it hanging down her back, then she donned the oversized shirt which reached to mid-thigh and suitably disguised every scrap of her body.

This time she would not allow her emotions to ambush all her good intentions. She would smile on the surface and eventually the smiles would become a part of her expression whenever she was in his company.

She stared at the reflection in the mirror and practised a smile.

By the time he returned with a tray, she was back in bed and under the covers.

'You look better,' he said, glancing at her and looking away. 'Food.'

'You shouldn't have,' Jessica said politely as he placed the tray on her lap and, mysteriously, resumed his position on the chair next to the bed.

'You're absolutely right. I should have just let you fend for yourself.'

'Well, I've done it all my life,' she answered absent-mindedly, tucking into a mound of scrambled egg and toast. Her hair slipped over a shoulder and she flicked it back, thinking that she should have tied the lot into a ponytail.

'Sounds exhausting,' he said eventually, and she stopped eating momentarily to look across at him.

'What does?'

'A lifetime of fending for yourself.'

Jessica flushed and resumed eating. This was normal conversation, she told herself. Getting uptight was only going to drag her back to square one, back to the place where every word he uttered had the ability to throw her off balance.

Step one in learning how to deal with her situation would be to answer his questions courteously and without flinching.

'Oh, it becomes a habit after a while,' she said airily. 'This tastes delicious, by the way. I've always admired a man who's not afraid of cooking.'

'Well, I personally wouldn't call two scrambled eggs the epitome of haute cuisine.'

'Small beginnings,' Jessica said, finishing the very last morsel and closing her knife and fork with some regret. Then she rested back against the pillows with her cup of tea and watched in silence as he removed the tray from bed to side table.

'There's no need for you to stay here, you know,' she said eventually, when he showed no signs of moving. 'I give you my word that I won't leave the room and hurtle outside in another fit of confusion.'

'Was that why you did it?' he asked softly. 'Because my touching you confused you?'

The sudden intimacy of the question wedged a splinter in her determined effort to keep up a smiling façade. She felt the smile begin to slip a little.

'I mean,' she said, disregarding his question, 'haven't you got some work to do? The odd fax to send somewhere?'

'Nothing that can't wait.' He paused and continued staring at her. 'You haven't answered my question.'

'There's nothing *to* answer.' She could feel her heart beating very quickly. Doing double time.

'What if I said that I would never lay another finger on you again?' A dark flush had spread across his face and he threw her a challenging look from under his lashes.

'I don't understand what you're saying.'

'We can simply live under the same roof.'

'It would drive me crazy!' Jessica blurted out. Tears were beginning to prick the backs of her eyes. How was she supposed to get all her defences in place, if he wasn't prepared to play the game according to her rules?

'I get the message.' He stood up abruptly and looked down at her with his hands in his pockets.

'You don't understand!' Imploring eyes met cold ice.

'I think I do. Forget I ever asked the question. You were right. I have work to do, so I'll leave you here to get on with your resting. Tonight, I'll give my mother a call and she can come up and lend a hand.'

'Your mother?'

'Good night, Jessica. Call me if you need anything. I'll be in the office downstairs.'

'Wait, Bruno.' He was already heading to the door. 'Why don't we talk about this?' She could feel herself on the verge of confessing everything to him and hang the consequences.

'There's nothing to talk about,' he said politely. 'Let's not go along the road of forcing something that's just not there. We're two people who happened to meet in passing, which, as you've been at great pains to point out, is precisely where it should have been left.'

With that he left the room, and Jessica crumpled back onto the bed. It was over. There had been a finality in his voice when he had spoken and beyond them now was nothing. He had made one last effort to accommodate her because of the baby, and she had spontaneously uttered the wrong words. Not that there would have been any right ones.

The past and the present tangled together in her head and she switched the overhead light off, waiting, dry-eyed, as the sky outside darkened. There were no noises in the house, and she wouldn't have been surprised to find that he had gone out. Gone to find himself a real woman, instead of a repressed, inhibited one who couldn't even say what was in her mind because heartfelt truths were something she had never felt the need to indulge in before.

When she next opened her eyes, it was to find light trying to get through the curtain, and there was a knocking on the bedroom door. She wasn't entirely sure which had awakened her. The light or the sound of knocking. Her watch, which she was still wearing, showed her that it was a little after eight.

The shirt—crumpled. The hair—a mess. The face—she daredn't look. If Bruno wasn't repelled by her enough already, then he was in for a treat.

She watched the door handle being turned, frantically tried to arrange her face into something loosely resembling a human being instead of a zombie recently roused from the local graveyard, and was already wearing a fixed, if jaw-aching, smile on her lips when a tall, dark-haired woman entered the room. She was dressed smartly in a tan-coloured cashmere twin set although, instead of the customary pearls, she wore three long strands of gold around her neck.

If this is the housekeeper, then I'm the Queen of England, Jessica thought, but she kept smiling until the woman approached the bed.

It then occurred to her that the constant smile might look a bit manic and she allowed her mouth to relax a little.

'You must be wondering who I am,' the woman said, and as soon as she had spoken Jessica knew precisely who the woman was. Right age, right look, right accent. Her heart sank.

'You must be Bruno's mother,' she said, feeling at a

disadvantage in her son's shirt, in bed. This sort of elegant, well-bred woman was best dealt with on fairly equal terms. The fact of the pregnancy was just another huge, added disadvantage. The woman had the same angular, strong face as her son although time had weathered it into something slightly less daunting.

'Victoria.' She stepped into the room, and, if she was horrified at the circumstances that had brought her to London from the sanity of her country mansion, then she showed no sign of it. 'And you're Jessica, of course.'

'I'm very pleased to meet you,' Jessica lied.

'Are you?' The bright, shrewd eyes examined her. 'I wish I could say the same but I'm very much afraid that it would be a complete lie.'

Okay, Jessica thought. Let's not beat about the bush here.

'I came up last night, actually, on Bruno's request. He's going to be out of the country for a few days and he thought that, in view of the situation, my presence here might be a help.'

Jessica nodded miserably, at a loss for words.

'You have no experience of children, as yet, but, speaking as a mother, I needn't tell you how disappointed I am with this situation.'

'Well,' Jessica said, firing on a few cylinders now that the immediate shock had worn off, 'and I would hate to appear rude, but, speaking as the person in the middle of the situation, I can assure you that it's not exactly a bed of roses for me either.'

For the first time, a glimmer of humour flitted across the woman's face, but she remained silent for a while, eventually moving to pull back the curtains, then to sit in still repose on the love chair by the bay window. Jessica followed her warily with her eyes.

'I had always expected, my dear, that Bruno would indulge his mother with a white wedding, with all the trimmings...' She smiled a little wistfully. 'No, perhaps not quite the full affair, but a wedding, at any rate.'

'I understand,' Jessica said uncomfortably. Had he told his mother that a wedding had been planned? Planned and then dismantled in the blink of an eye?

'He tells me that any such thing is out of the question.' She paused and looked carefully at Jessica. 'May I ask why?'

'Because weddings, marriage... I was a fool, Mrs Carr. A mistake and...' Her voice was beginning to go. She could feel her throat seizing up, but she forced herself to plough on. 'And here I am. Pregnant. I know that Bruno hadn't planned for his life to take this awkward course, and I certainly hadn't.'

'What *had* you planned, my dear?' The voice was soft but insistent, and Jessica sighed and lay back on the bed, with her eyes on the ceiling.

What *had* she planned? It was a good question.

'I'd planned a life of independence. A career. A life with no emotional involvement. I always thought that it would just be so much easier. I certainly hadn't planned on babies and on your son... No, all that had been the last thing on my mind...'

'All that?'

Jessica shifted her head so that she was looking at Bruno's mother. She shrugged. 'Involvement, I guess. I know there's a baby, but marriage...well, underneath it all, I guess I was more of a foolish romantic than I'd believed. I guess I'd thought all along that marriage and love needed to go together. Bruno and I won't be married because he doesn't love me, and I can't think of anything more unfair on him than shackling him to my side because of a mistake.'

'Unfair on you as well, if you don't love him either.'

Jessica caught the woman's eyes and opened her mouth to agree but found that she couldn't. No more lies.

'If only it was as easy as that,' she murmured, half to herself. 'If only.'

# CHAPTER TEN

IT WAS after midnight when banging on the front door dragged Jessica out of her sleep. For the first time since returning to her own place two days ago, she cursed the fact that she was no longer under Bruno Carr's roof, because if she had been there would have been no chance of hearing anyone knock or bang or possibly even break down his front door.

As it was, she yawned and staggered into her dressing gown and then headed to the door, which she opened by a couple of inches, making sure to keep the chain firmly in place. She lived in a relatively safe part of town, but it still didn't make sense to take chances, especially at this hour, notorious for drunken revellers heading home, only stopping off *en route* to cause a bit of random harassment.

The minute she saw who was standing outside her front door, all signs of sleep vanished.

'Open this door,' Bruno commanded, looking as though he might risk pushing it with his shoulder, despite the obstacle of the chain. He was dressed, mysteriously at this hour, in his work suit, although his tie was askew as though he had been tugging it down.

'What are you doing here at this hour? I thought you weren't going to be back in the country for another three days.'

'Plans changed.'

'In that case you can find your way back to your own house. Do you realise what time it is? I was asleep!' She didn't add that it had taken her long enough to get to sleep in the first place without having what little she had enjoyed ruined halfway through.

'I don't care if you were levitating six inches off the bed, Jessica. Open this door or else I'll break the thing down.'

'You're not strong enough,' she pointed out flatly.

'In which case, I'll yell so loudly that every neighbour in a sixty-mile radius will come running to see what's going on.'

She didn't doubt him either. She reluctantly unhooked the chain from the door and stood aside to let him enter. His absence over the past five days had been just what she'd needed to put him in perspective. Or so she reminded herself as she watched him divest himself of his jacket and stride purposefully towards her sitting room. The fact that it was after twelve o'clock was obviously something that hadn't registered with him, or maybe his body was still running on American time.

'So,' she said mutinously, following him into the sitting room, but then standing by the door with her arms folded defensively. 'What do you want?'

'I had a long chat with my mother when I got back from America this evening,' he said, perching on the window-ledge and staring at her, his eyes hooded and unrevealing.

'And? What does that have to do with me? I'm tired, and whatever you have to say to me can wait until another day.' Her sluggish brain began working furiously, trying to remember what she could possibly have said to his mother that might have been relayed back to him, but she had been very careful to keep her emotions to herself. Even when it had become patently clear that she and his mother got along really rather well, circumstances considering. Despite frequent references to maternal disapproval, there was something innately warm inside Victoria that Jessica had found

herself responding to. So what could she have told her son
that had made him find his way over here at this hour?

'I liked your mother!' she blurted out, confused. 'And I
thought she liked me too!'

'And you're wondering how she might have betrayed
one of your little confidences?' he said in a jeering voice.

'I didn't give her any!' Jessica retorted, whitening. Had
she? She had been tempted, but she had held back, biting
back the need to confess how she really felt about her son.
She wrapped her dressing gown more tightly around her,
but even so she still felt cold.

'Then why are you so frantic to try and remember what
you said to her? No, don't bother to answer that. Not that
you would. Denial is your instinctive response to any question you find even remotely troublesome.' He moved across
to one of the chairs and sat down, rubbing his eyes.

'Why are you sitting down and making yourself at home
at this hour of the morning?' Jessica asked coldly.

'I told you. We need to talk.'

'We've already talked. I don't remember it getting us
anywhere.'

'My mother liked you. Have I mentioned that?'

'You've been drinking, haven't you?' Jessica asked,
looking at him narrowly. He hadn't staggered into the
house like a typical inebriate, and his words weren't slur-
ring, but there was something aggressive and unpredictable
about his behaviour.

'Don't try and change the bloody topic, Jessica. I'm sick
to death of that ploy of yours. I'm sick of pussyfooting
around all your little problems.'

'You? Pussyfooting? Don't make me laugh. I'm going
to go and get you a cup of black coffee. You're going to
drink it and then you're going to leave.' She didn't give
him time to answer. Instead she swept out of the room,

headed towards the kitchen, relieved to find that he hadn't followed her, and then slumped heavily against the fridge door while she waited for the kettle to boil.

Why had he come? She had never seen him under the influence of drink, but she was pretty certain he was there now, whatever he might say, and drunks were notoriously unreliable. They said what was in their mind, and she didn't think that she could stand an hour's worth of Bruno Carr raving on about all her inadequacies. But how could she get him out? He was bigger than her and stronger and if he decided to stay put until he had said whatever piece he had come to say, then he would stay put.

The kettle began to boil and she shakily poured the water into a mug and then stirred in two heaped teaspoons of strong coffee granules.

She half expected to find that he had passed out on the sofa in her absence, but when she got back to the sitting room it was to find him where she had left him, and if the drink was getting to him then he showed zero signs of it.

'Drink up.' She stood over him with her arms folded and watched as he took a mouthful and then recoiled, spluttering.

'What the hell have you put in this?'

'You've had too much to drink. The stronger the coffee, the better,' she told him calmly, and he muttered something unflattering under his breath. 'You need to get back to your house, get yourself into bed with a couple of paracetamol and go to sleep. In the morning, you might be coherent.' And you won't be here, she thought to herself. Whatever state he was in, she still didn't like what he could do to her. Just seeing him, looking down at that rumpled thatch of black hair, was enough to make her feel unsteady.

'Stop giving orders. I'm sick to death of you giving orders.'

'You're sick of a lot of things concerning me, aren't you? Is that why you came here? So that you could tell me just how sick you are of me and everything that I do and say? I wouldn't have thought that you would need drink as a prop to give you Dutch courage for that, though. You've always been just fine at telling me precisely what you think.'

'Oh, do me a favour. You're hardly the shrinking violet when it comes to saying what's on your mind.'

'Right, I'm off to bed.' She made a move to turn away and he grabbed her clumsily by the wrist.

'Oh, no, you don't. You're going to stay right here and listen to what I have to say.' He frowned, as though he had temporarily forgotten what he had to say, and Jessica watched him with an expression of long-suffering patience.

'Then hurry up and say it. I'm tired.'

'No, you're not. You're all wired up because I'm here.' He shot her a crafty look from under his lashes, which she did her best to ignore, but her heart had gone into overdrive.

'Don't flatter yourself.'

'I'm not.' He gave her a lopsided, knowing smile and she raised her eyebrows expressively.

'And that wolfish grin doesn't sit well on someone who's had too much to drink. You just look ridiculous.' The annoying thing was that he looked anything but ridiculous, even though he should have. 'And I don't recall saying anything funny,' she snapped, when he grinned delightedly at this remark.

'Did I tell you that my mother took to you?'

'Yes, as a matter of fact, you did.'

'Said you had a lot of fighting spirit.' He gave something that sounded like a snort. 'What could I do but agree with her?'

He was still loosely hanging on to her wrist as though

having forgotten that his hand was there, and she tried to jerk her hand away. Instantly, his grip tightened, though he was still staring thoughtfully into the distance.

'Would you mind letting me go?'

'Only if you promise not to hover over me like a school-teacher with your arms folded.'

She sighed loudly and nodded, then, when he continued looking at her, repeated woodenly, 'I promise not to hover over you like a schoolteacher with my arms folded.' At which he gave her a satisfied look, released her hand, and she gratefully went to the sofa and sat down, curling her legs underneath her.

'My mother never really cared for the women I've gone out with,' he said in a ruminating voice.

'Yes. I know.'

'You *know*?'

'She told me.' That, Jessica freely admitted to herself, had given her a buzz.

'And what *precisely* did she tell you?'

'She *precisely* told me that you always went for the same type of woman. Pretty, empty-headed, disposable.'

'My mother told you all that, did she?' His voice was blustering, but she could see that he was severely taken aback. 'So you two sat there, having cosy little confidential chit-chats at my expense over cups of tea.'

'Your name cropped up now and again.' Jessica shrugged. 'Bound to, I guess, under the circumstances.'

'And what other gems did she come up with?'

'She said that when you were three you rifled her lipstick drawer, smeared bright red lipstick all over your face and then fell down the stairs in her high-heeled shoes.' That had been such a gem of a confidence that she couldn't resist smiling now at the image, and Bruno scowled at her.

'God, the woman never lets me forget embarrassing incidents like that. I was three at the time!'

'That's probably because you've managed to put all embarrassing incidents behind you now.'

'Well, it would be extremely suspect if I was still prone to smearing lipstick on my face and tripping downstairs in high-heeled shoes, wouldn't it?'

'Anyway, we're getting off the topic of why you're here.' She felt she had to drag the conversation back into the boxing ring or else totally lose sight of the fact that Bruno Carr was to be kept at a safe distance.

'So we are.' He stretched his feet out and crossed them at the ankles, then he clasped his hands behind his head and sank into silence.

'Well?' Jessica prompted.

'My mother didn't expect to like you. When I first explained the situation to her on the telephone, she was horrified. 'Course, she blamed you for the whole mess.'

'Oh, of course,' Jessica said sarcastically. 'Because Archangel Bruno couldn't possibly have had a hand in it at all!'

'It seems she changed her mind after meeting you.'

'You mean...she thinks that you might be partly responsible for the situation? You amaze me!'

'I mean she expected to find that you followed the trend of my usual girlfriends.'

'Ah!' She was no clearer now as to the direction this conversation was going but she realised that she couldn't have halted it even if she wanted to. Which she didn't.

'Don't interrupt,' he ordered and she declined to point out that she hadn't. 'I came here fortified to say my speech and you'll sit there and listen to it. My mother...whom I love dearly and whose opinions I value greatly, seemed to think...' His voice petered out and he frowned accusingly at her, as though she were personally responsible for his failure to carry on.

'I haven't interrupted,' Jessica pointed out. 'You were saying…?'

'She seemed to think that you might possibly be the right woman for me.'

Jessica's mouth dropped open in sheer amazement. If his mother had told him that, then the woman was an actress of Oscar-winning standards because she had certainly said nothing to Jessica of the sort. In fact, she had pointedly steered clear of any matchmaking tendencies.

'She seems to think I might be better off with someone like you.'

'*Someone like me?* I'm not an act at a circus show! What do you mean *someone like me*? I can't think that your mother would have referred to me in those terms!' Her eyes started welling up and she blinked the tears back.

'No, she didn't. God!' He stood up and raked his fingers through his hair and began pacing the room as if he needed the physical activity to think better. 'You're not making this any easier for me,' he said, stopping in front of her. Looming so that she had to look up at him.

'She seemed to think that you and I are rather well suited, which happens to be my opinion as well.' Jessica opened her mouth and he held up one hand for her to be quiet, then he sat down heavily next to her on the sofa. 'And it has nothing to do with the baby. Well, obviously the baby comes into the equation. The fact is I happen to enjoy your company even if *you* spend half your time running away from my questions and the other half giving me a hard time for asking them in the first place.'

Jessica could feel her heart beating quicker and quicker, and she thought that she might well be holding her breath, so she exhaled very deeply and told herself not to get worked up over what he was saying because it probably wasn't leading where she would dearly have wanted it to lead.

'Well?' he prompted challengingly. 'Aren't you going to rush in here to defend yourself?'

'I'll wait until you reach the end of your speech. I wouldn't want to be accused of interrupting you.'

'There you go again! Throwing me off my stride!' He glared at her. 'You've done that from day one! I'm not accustomed to having to be alert one hundred per cent of the time when I'm with a woman, just in case some stray verbal arrow comes flying my way!'

'I *know* what you've been accustomed to, Bruno. Isn't that why marriage would never work between us? Because you're not accustomed to women like me? Because at the end of the day, whatever your mother says and however much your head agrees with her, your heart is firmly rooted in another type of girl?'

'So I've told myself for the past few weeks,' he muttered, and she strained across to hear what he was saying.

'What was that?'

'You heard me!' He looked at her, tilted his head slightly to one side and gave her a winningly boyish 'can't you see where I'm heading?' look, which she returned with a perplexed frown.

'It seems that I rather like the intelligent, bossy—'

'I am not bossy!'

'Answer-me-back at the drop of a hat style of woman.'

Jessica, listening intently to every word, found that she was having trouble swallowing. Her throat appeared to have become very dry.

'It seems that…' he began, and then, once more, left the sentence unfinished.

'I wish you'd get to the point, Bruno.'

'Because you can't wait to see the back of me?'

'No.'

'Are you telling me that you don't want me to go?' He gave her a sly, charming smile and she flushed. 'My mother informed me that she thinks you're not quite as hostile towards me as you like to make out...'

'Oh, she does, does she?' Traitor, Jessica thought.

'Yes. What do you say?'

'Oh, what does it matter?' she said on a sigh. 'It doesn't matter how many roads we go down, we always seem to end up right back at the place we started, which, in case you're wondering, is nowhere.'

'I disagree. Have I told you that I've been doing some thinking?'

'I think you might have.'

'I don't repulse you, do I, Jessica? Admit it. It's just the opposite, isn't it? I turn you on and that terrifies you. That's why you didn't want to continue what we had once we got back to England. That's why you've been fighting me every inch of the way. Because you're not indifferent to me at all. Okay, I'm going to lay all my cards on the table and tell you that I think you—'

'Don't you dare say it!' She felt the customary panic at the prospect of having her emotions laid bare for him to pick over, but hard on the heels of panic came a kind of weary lassitude. She was fed up playing games. What was the point of it all? It didn't change the way she felt.

'Why not? Because you might give yourself away?'

'Is that why you came over here, Bruno?' she asked quietly. 'So that you can gloat at yet another conquest?'

He looked at her startled, then confused, but she was too dispirited to react to the fact that he had just pulled off the greatest piece of bluffing he had probably ever done in his life.

'No, that's not why I came here.'

Jessica looked at him, mildly surprised at this admission.

'I came here to tell you that…it seems that…well, my mother put two and two together to be honest…nothing better to do with her time than try and analyse other people's motivations… I don't suppose you have a glass of whisky lying about, do you?' When she shook her head, he continued, flushing, 'If you really want to know, I think you've managed to pull the rug from under my feet…'

'Rug? What rug? What on earth are you on about?'

'You've made me fall in love with you.' He stared at her defiantly, and his admission was so overwhelming that for a few seconds she sat there and stared back at him with her lips parted. 'I couldn't stop thinking about you when I got back to England. I was pretty sure that you'd make contact, and when nothing happened I told myself that it didn't matter. In fact, that it was the best thing that could happen. I tried to launch myself back into my social life, I even dated a couple of other women, but it was a ridiculous farce. I compared all of them to you, and I missed you.'

'You *slept* with other women?'

'I don't think I could have even if I'd wanted to,' he replied with a dry, ironic laugh. 'How could I when my head was filled with you?'

Jessica could feel a foolish grin spread over her face.

'Good,' she told him comfortably. 'Carry on.'

'*Good?*' He shifted slightly. ''Course, I'm only admitting all this because I know you feel precisely the same way about me…don't you?' He paused. 'Don't you?'

'I…well, yes…I do happen to like you very much…' She smiled to herself.

'*Like?*'

'Perhaps a bit more.'

'You mean you're deeply, irretrievably, passionately in love with me?'

Jessica laughed and gazed at him tenderly. She inched her way towards him until she was curled against him, and could hear the beating of his heart through his shirt. He kissed her hair and stroked it, then kissed it again.

'I might well be,' she said softly. 'You might well have pulled the rug from under my feet as well.' She raised her face to his and her heart, which had been doing all sorts of odd things ever since he had appeared on the scene, seemed to settle in just the place it belonged. 'I thought I could do without men and I could. I just found that I couldn't do without you.'

'What do you mean by that?' he asked in mock hurt, kissing the tip of her nose while he stroked her neck very gently. 'I'm not an act at a circus show, you know.'

'I couldn't bear the thought of marrying you when you didn't love me and I couldn't bear the thought of leaving you, of only being tied to you through our child.'

He smiled and kissed her very thoroughly on the mouth and she moaned and guided his hand to her breast.

'So. Will you marry me?' he asked huskily.

'Do you know, Bruno Carr? I think I just might.'

# EPILOGUE

'MUMMY! Mummy! Mummy!'

Jessica looked at her daughter and against the flickering night shadows she could make out the glowing eyes and rosy-cheeked smile. Beyond her, she met Bruno's eyes and they smiled at one another. With Amy in his arms, her little face was at the same level as his, and even without the benefit of bright lights it was easy for her to see how closely they resembled each other.

'Strong genes,' he had told her with proud satisfaction two years ago when he had gazed down at that seven-pound three-ounce scrap of closed-fisted baby wrapped in blankets. 'Spit image of me. A little clone.'

'Poor child!' Jessica had teased, looking at the thatch of dark hair.

'Amy! Amy! Amy!' Jessica replied, reaching to stroke her daughter's face. It was after seven and they had wrapped her up warmly for this little expedition to the local village school.

'Isn't she a little nag?' Bruno murmured, nuzzling Amy's cheek with his nose and then planting a kiss on her neck. 'I knew she'd inherited certain important character traits from you!'

Jessica laughed, and wondered, not for the first time, how she could still be so thrilled with this extraordinary man. She still felt that magical tingle of awareness whenever he was near her and that warm feeling of security, as though the sweetest things in life had somehow found her and were there to stay.

'Me like de fireworks!'

'I can see that you do, darling.'

'She's so *advanced*,' Bruno said in wonderment, for the umpteenth time, and Jessica's arm around his waist circled him even closer.

'You're biased.'

'Not at all. How many children of her age do you know can hold a conversation?'

Jessica doubted whether her daughter's ability to string words together could actually be labelled 'holding a conversation' but she knew better than to argue the point. Bruno, the archetypal single man, had become the most devoted father.

'Absolutely none,' she agreed and she saw the glimmer of teeth as he smiled and looked upwards to where a shower of light was descending back to earth. The ground was packed to the rafters, but here, at the back, it was as though there were only the three of them in the entire universe. Amy's face, tilted upwards, was alight with childish amazement.

'Again!' she cried. 'Again! Again! Again!'

'Time to go, Amy,' Jessica said, laughing, as her daughter pushed out her mouth in stubborn disagreement.

'No!'

They walked past groups of milling people towards the car and, despite the childish protestations and tears, within five minutes Amy was sound asleep, her thumb half falling out of her mouth, her head curled to one side.

'Isn't she an angel when she's asleep?' Jessica said, resting her head back and half closing her eyes.

'Something else she's inherited from you,' Bruno said softly. She felt his hand cover hers and their fingers entwined into a solid bond. 'Now admit it, aren't you glad you persuaded me to marry you?'

She laughed and squeezed his fingers. 'Oh, yes, my lord and master!'

'And, of course, you can prove that when we get back,' he growled, and then he shook his head. 'But then again, maybe not. Not quite yet, anyway.'

'I know. Things *are* getting a trifle difficult on that front, aren't they, my love?' she said ruefully, glancing down at her stomach.

'And a more beautiful reason for that I can't imagine.' He smiled and glanced across to her, his eyes warm and loving. 'Just think, by Christmas, no more stomach.'

'I know,' she sighed contentedly. 'But lots of broken nights.'

'Could things be better?'

And they laughed in unison.

# Celebrate **15** years with

 **HARLEQUIN®**
*Makes any time special* ™

 **WIN A DREAM**

# In celebration of Harlequin®'s golden anniversary

Enter to win a *dream!* You could win:

- A luxurious trip for two to
*The Renaissance Cottonwoods Resort*
in Scottsdale, Arizona, or

- A bouquet of flowers once a week for a year
from **FTD**, or

- A $500 shopping spree, or

- A fabulous bath & body gift basket, including
**K-tel's** *Candlelight and Romance* 5-CD set.

Look for **WIN A DREAM** flash on
specially marked Harlequin® titles by
Penny Jordan, Dallas Schulze,
Anne Stuart and Kristine Rolofson
in October 1999*.

**FTD**

**RENAISSANCE.**
**COTTONWOODS RESORT**
SCOTTSDALE, ARIZONA

**K·TEL**

*No purchase necessary—for contest details send a self-addressed envelope to
Harlequin Makes Any Time Special Contest, P.O. Box 9069, Buffalo, NY, 14269-9069
(include contest name on self-addressed envelope). Contest ends December 31, 1999.
Open to U.S. and Canadian residents who are 18 or over. Void where prohibited.

PHMATS-GR

# Coming Next Month

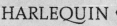 

HARLEQUIN PRESENTS®

## THE BEST HAS JUST GOTTEN BETTER!

**#2049 MISTRESS BY ARRANGEMENT Helen Bianchin
(Presents Passion)**
Michelle is stunned when wealthy businessman
Nikos Alessandros asks her to be his social companion for a
few weeks. Will Michelle, under pressure from her family to
make a suitable marriage, find herself becoming a mistress
by arrangement?

**#2050 HAVING LEO'S CHILD Emma Darcy
(Expecting!)**
Leo insisted she marry him for the sake of their unborn child.
But despite his fiery kisses, Teri couldn't forget that Leo had
never considered marrying her before she got pregnant.
Could they turn great sex into eternal love?

**#2051 TO BE A BRIDEGROOM Carole Mortimer
(Bachelor Brothers)**
Jordan is the youngest Hunter brother. His devilish good
looks have helped him seduce any woman he's ever wanted—
except Stazy. There's only one way for Jordan to get to the
head of Stazy's queue—become a bridegroom!

**#2052 A HUSBAND OF CONVENIENCE Jacqueline Baird**
When an accident left Josie with amnesia, she assumed that
her gorgeous husband, Conan, was the father of her unborn
baby. They shared passionate nights until she remembered
that theirs was actually a marriage of convenience....

**#2053 WEDDING-NIGHT BABY Kim Lawrence**
Georgina decided she couldn't attend her ex-fiancé's wedding alone—she needed an escort! Callum Stewart was
perfect: gorgeous, dynamic...and on the night of the
wedding he became the father of her child!

**#2054 THE IMPATIENT GROOM Sara Wood
(Society Weddings)**
Prince Rozzano di Barsini whisked Sophia Charlton away to
Venice in his private jet. One whirlwind seduction later, she'd
agreed to be his bride. But why was Rozzano in such a hurry
to marry? Because he needed an heir...?